"You're not listening to me. We don't even know enough about each other to fool anyone."

Nick caught her in his arms. "I'm listening. I'm ignoring what you have to say. We will make this work. Too much depends on it."

"But…" She'd scarcely opened her mouth to protest when Nick covered her lips with his, successfully stopping any argument Molly might have voiced.

She stood in his embrace, quickly feeling her defenses melt as his kiss went on and on. His lips were warm and firm, and expert at drawing a response.

Endless time later he pulled back and looked at her, satisfaction reflected in his gaze. "Now you look kissed."

ISBN 0-373-03822-4

HIS CONVENIENT FIANCÉE

First North American Publication 2004.

This edition published by arrangement with Harlequin Books S.A.

www.eHarlequin.com

Printed in U.S.A.

HIS CONVENIENT FIANCÉE

Barbara McMahon

TORONTO • NEW YORK • LONDON
AMSTERDAM • PARIS • SYDNEY • HAMBURG
STOCKHOLM • ATHENS • TOKYO • MILAN • MADRID
PRAGUE • WARSAW • BUDAPEST • AUCKLAND

CHAPTER ONE

MOLLY knew she was stalling. As she paced the crowded sidewalk in front of the Magellan Hotel on trendy Union Square, her thoughts flew in a thousand different directions. She did not want to go up to the reception. Yet to avoid it would be cowardly. And give rise to even more talk. She'd been the victim of enough gossip for the last three months. She really, really didn't want to add to it today!

Another cab swerved to a stop before the hotel's main entrance and when the uniformed doorman stepped to the curb to open the door, Molly recognized Harold Satten and his wife. He was one of Justin's cohorts—a fellow account executive at the firm they all worked for, Zentech. Just her luck they spotted her at almost the same time she saw them. Another couple on their way to the Zentech event. The same event she should have arrived at some ten minutes ago.

"Hello, Molly. This is the place, isn't it?" Harold asked, joining her on the sidewalk.

"On the twenty-fifth floor," she confirmed, smiling a polite acknowledgment to Harold's wife.

"Shall we go?" he asked.

"I'm waiting for someone," Molly replied, the lie rolling off her lips with unaccustomed ease.

"Oh, I thought you were alone."

Sheesh, she thought, refraining from making a face

with effort. Did the entire world know about the big breakup? Well, of course they did. Brittany made sure of that. Poor Molly. Brittany hadn't *meant* to come between Molly and Justin, but when they fell in love, what were they to do, she asked anyone within earshot—usually when Molly could also overhear.

"No, I'm waiting for someone," she repeated, glancing up the busy street as if seeking a familiar face.

"We'll see you up there, then," Harold said.

Holding her fake, polite smile until they were out of sight, Molly sighed. Yes, they would see her. It was a command appearance. And ordinarily she would have been thrilled. It was her design concept, after all, and her innovative ideas for the account that had been the pivotal point in signing one of Japan's huge conglomerates, Hamakomoto Industries, to the lucrative contract. Steve Powers was the account executive, but it was her artwork that had clinched the deal.

And hadn't that made Brittany furious? The two women were both with the art department of Zentech, a high-tech, full service company that led the way in innovative concepts for businesses. And from the first day Molly had started, Brittany Taylor had had it in for her.

After almost seven years, Molly would have thought she'd have grown immune. But Brittany's deliberately luring Justin had been the final straw. Molly would not give in to the pitying glances and murmured condolences on her breakup with Justin. No more miss nice girl, she was fighting back!

The celebratory reception had started ten minutes

ago. The press, media and important and influential movers and shakers of San Francisco were on the impressive guest list. Everyone who was anyone would be there.

Including Justin Morris—and Brittany.

Molly walked a few feet along the sidewalk, ideas spinning. Maybe she could disappear for a couple of weeks, and then tell them at work she'd been kidnapped by aliens. Or maybe she could fake a fall and sprained ankle. She eyed the dirty cement with distaste. Not such a good idea.

Or maybe she could pull off the idea her neighbor Shelly had come up with—pretend she was engaged and her fiancé hadn't been able to make the event. Harold could attest to her pacing the sidewalk as if she were impatiently awaiting someone.

It was pathetic. She was probably the only woman in San Francisco who couldn't come up with a date for a business reception. But most of the people she knew well enough to ask, also worked at Zentech. The last thing she wanted to do was have anyone there know she was thinking of subterfuge to minimize damage from Brittany's latest attack.

Ordinarily going alone to a company event wouldn't matter a bit. But that was before last week's conference where Brittany had cast aspersions on Molly's ability to stick to a long-term project—as witnessed by her flighty behavior with relationships. As if Molly had been the one to dump Justin.

Molly ground her teeth just thinking about Brittany's smarmy sweetness and the others around the table, glancing between them. She knew, of course, it was professional jealousy. Brittany's last several design concepts had not been accepted, where Molly's had. But knowing didn't help.

Four months ago Molly had been thinking wedding bells. Justin had been dating Brittany on the sly. Molly's fantasies had fizzled instantly when she learned the truth. If he wanted Brittany Taylor, he was welcome to her! They deserved each other.

The worst of it, however, was the fact she, Justin and Brittany all worked for the same company. Everyone had seen Molly and Justin as a couple at the Christmas party. And everyone knew, thanks to Brittany, that she and Justin were now the romance of the century.

Molly frowned. She hated feeling like the dumped also-ran while Justin paraded around with super sweet Brittany.

"Stupid, stupid, stupid," she muttered. She should have known better than to even think about dating a coworker. Every time she saw him in the halls of Zentech, she was reminded again of the way he played around and that she'd only been one of many. Brittany would most likely be on the receiving end one day, but not today.

Now Molly was expected to show up at the reception and act as if life was great. Of course no one else had to face Justin and the oh-so-stunning Brittany and pretend it didn't matter. Taking a deep breath, Molly faced the hotel. She'd give it her best shot.

Glancing around one last time as if expecting a miracle, she realized unless she dragged a perfect stranger up to the reception, she was going to show up alone. Time to put on the ring she'd brought and brazen it out.

Except she suspected Brittany would see right through the scheme. The woman was not one to sit around silently and let others get on with their lives. She liked to gloat.

Anger touched her. If Justin had been any kind of friend, he would have stayed away from today's event. It should have been her shining moment. Instead, she had an ex-boyfriend everyone knew about and his new smug girlfriend hogging the spotlight.

She'd heard the rumors flying around the office over the last few weeks. Seen the sly speculative looks from coworkers. Felt the sympathetic glances. She'd been caught up in the art layout and design for Hamakomoto, but not to the exclusion of coming up for air and noticing what was going on from time to time.

Hoping she could pull it off, she needed to save face in front of all of the influential businessmen. She raised her chin and marched directly into the lavish lobby of the hotel. A discreet sign to the left caught her eye. *Magellan's Pub.* Ah, maybe a bit of Dutch courage would help.

She entered the dimly lit space and gazed around. Except for a couple looking like honeymooners sitting at a table against the wall, and a man leaning against the far end of the bar talking with the bartender, the place was empty. Obviously too early for most serious drinkers.

She walked to the gleaming mahogany bar and perched gingerly on a high stool. The bartender left his conversation and headed her way.

"What can I get you?" His smile was friendly.

Probably because he doesn't know about Brittany, Molly thought glumly. She could just imagine it turning sympathetic if he knew her situation.

"I'll have a gin and tonic. No, wait, I hate gin. Give me bourbon straight up. No, wait, I don't like that, either. Maybe a nice glass of Chardonnay. No, wait, would that be enough? How about a rum and Coke? No, wait, I always had that with Justin, bad association. Damn!"

"So what do you really want?" the bartender asked.

"What I really, really want is something tall, dark and dangerous," Molly said morosely, wishing she could order up a temporary fiancé as easily as she could a drink. She glanced at her watch. It was almost four-thirty. If she didn't get up there soon, her tardiness would have an even greater impact. She could imagine the gossip running rampant.

"How about blond and friendly?" he countered.

"What?" She looked up into bright blue eyes beneath a blond mop. The man looked as cute as could be. But not the stuff of romance.

"Nope, tall dark and dangerous or none at all. I'll have a rum and Coke." She couldn't avoid the only drink she really liked the rest of her life because of Justin.

The bartender began to prepare the beverage, eyeing her as he did so. "Trouble?"

"Does everyone who comes in here have troubles?"

"Only those who come in at four in the afternoon." He set her glass on a coaster in front of her.

"And I'm part psychologist you know, comes with the trade."

"Umm." She took a sip. Never much of a drinker, she wondered how much this would help. It wouldn't do to show up at her company's celebratory event fiancé-less and inebriated!

She glanced at her watch again. It was getting later by the minute. Was there already talk—instigated by Brittany, of course. She could just hear her sly innuendoes and see her wide-eyed innocent, sympathetic act. Molly wondered if she was up to facing another bout.

"Waiting for a date?" the bartender asked.

"I wish. I'm supposed to be upstairs at the Zentech reception on the 25th floor."

"I imagine drinks up there are free."

She sipped again, then opened her clutch purse. Taking out her grandmother's engagement ring she looked at it. Glancing at the bartender, she held it up. "If I wore this, would you think I was engaged?"

"Are you?"

"That's not the point. What would you think?"

"I'd think a pretty woman like you would be taken, engagement ring or not."

She blinked, smiled. "Wow, maybe blond and cute would work after all."

He winked at her and glanced at the other end of the bar. Molly looked down there and met a dark scowl. The man couldn't possibly hear them, he was too far away and the soft strains of background music muted other sounds. She studied him for a moment.

Now he would fit the bill. Tall, dark and decidedly dangerous. He looked like a pirate who had been poured into a business suit. He wasn't handsome exactly, his face was too rough-hewn for that. But there was a decidedly arrogant air about the man that would set Brittany back on her heels. Who was he? And why was he in a bar at four o'clock?

She looked back at her friendly bartender.

"He would work," she said whimsically.

"You think?"

"If he'd stop frowning long enough to look like a devoted fiancé. But I think I'll go with the ring and excuse."

"What excuse?"

"That something came up at the last minute and my darling fiancé couldn't make it after all."

"Why the need for a darling fiancé?" he asked leaning on the bar with one arm, apparently ready to listen for as long as it took.

She stared at her drink for a long moment, feeling once again the embarrassment Justin's deflection had caused. Odd, that was the only emotion she felt. Hadn't she loved him after all? She'd enjoyed being with him. They'd even talked of plans for marriage. Shouldn't she be brokenhearted?

Instead, she was embarrassed.

"To save face. Did you know the Japanese feel strongly about saving face?"

"How did we get to the Japanese?"

"There will be a number of Japanese people at the celebration. I know Mr. Yamamoto and Mr. Harishni. They liked my designs, you see. I have to attend. It just would be so much easier to face everyone with a fiancé in tow."

"Because?"

"Okay, Mr. Psychologist Bartender, it would be easier because the man I thought I was going to marry will be there today with his new girlfriend. I have done my best to avoid both of them for weeks, but it doesn't always work that way. I would so love to waltz in without a care in the world with someone extra special with me. Justin and Brittany work where I do, so everyone knows the situation and feels sorry for me." She frowned. "I hate that part."

"And the tall, dark and dangerous fiancé in tow would give you that extra cachet you'd need to pull off carefree?"

"Got it in one!"

The bartender laughed. "I have just the man for you. And maybe we can kill two birds with one stone. Hold on." He moved down to the other end of the bar.

Molly watched, fascinated. He wasn't really going to ask that tall, dark stranger to pose as her fiancé, was he? And even if he did, the man would never agree. He didn't look the type to agree to anything that didn't further his own enlightened self-interests.

She'd had it with corporate types who moved to their own agenda. Hadn't that been Justin to a T? At least in retrospect, she thought so. At the time, she'd been flattered by his attention. Now he treated her like a poor besotted fool who had misinterpreted his overtures of friendship. Ha! He'd been clear, but changed his tune when Brittany made her play—including pushing his projects through faster.

If she got involved anytime soon with someone else, she'd make sure he was friendly and nice and didn't have some secret desire to move ahead no matter who he stepped on.

And never again would she get involved with corporate types!

She watched as the bartender spoke to the other man, glancing back at her. Proposing her idea?

Mr. Tall Dark and Dangerous shook his head. No surprise there, though her heart dropped. Had she really held a glimmer of hope he'd agree?

She couldn't hear the words, but could see the bartender arguing the point. Something he said must have made an impression. The stranger studied her for a long moment, flicked a quick glance at his watch and then the door to the pub. He nodded once at the other man, stepped around the end of the bar and headed her way.

Molly's heart fluttered. Ohmygosh, was the man coming to talk with her? She clenched the ring tightly in her hand, her gaze fixed on him as he walked the length of the bar. She couldn't impose on a total stranger. She'd been joking when she said that to the bartender.

"I'm Nick Bailey. Donny said you needed an escort for the Zentech reception," he said, nodding toward the bartender.

She swallowed hard, was she really going to get tall, dark and dangerous? "Yes. No. Actually, I, uh, need, uh, *wanted* I mean, something more than just an escort. I need a temporary fiancé—just for tonight," she said all in a rush.

"All night?" He raised an eyebrow.

"Ohmygosh, no! Just for the reception upstairs, actually. It'll be over by eight at the latest."

He studied her a moment as if weighing her words. ''What exactly do you expect from a temporary fiancé?''

''Not much.'' She let her gaze run over him, her heart still acting weird. He was tall and immaculately dressed. The suit looked custom-made and expensive. His dark hair was well cut, his eyes steady and dark as they assessed her in return. She shivered at the reaction. He still looked like a pirate.

For a foolish moment, Molly was glad she looked her best. The new dress Shelly had talked her into was fashionable and fun—within acceptable business bounds. It was hard to know what to wear to business functions when she was used to paint-splattered jeans and tunics or shirts with chalk and charcoal dusting them.

But she had to hold her end up against Brittany!

She smiled up at him, feeling wildly reckless. ''Mostly you'd just have to stand around and look good. I think you'd do that perfectly. There'll be food and drinks on the house. I'd introduce you to various people, but you don't have to do anything really or say much. I could buy you dinner afterward if you like. As a thank-you.''

''So all I have to do is just be there?''

She nodded. He would be so perfect. He was taller than Justin, and ten times more masculine. His voice was deep and sexy, and he already had her fantasizing things a real fiancée would fantasize.

Oh, oh, maybe this wasn't such a great idea after all.

He glanced at the bartender in exasperation, then nodded at Molly. ''All right, I'll go with you. If you can wait a few more minutes.'' He glanced at his watch. ''I'm expecting someone.''

''You will?'' She, too, glanced at the bartender. He had the most peculiar smile on his face. ''Uh, why?'' Molly asked, afraid to believe her good fortune.

''Why not?''

''Well, you don't know me.''

''I hardly think you could do much in a room full of businessmen and women. You don't know me, either.''

''You don't look the type to do favors for strangers,'' she said bluntly.

''Not as a rule.'' He glanced at the bartender. ''But in this case, it'll help me out, as well.''

''Oh.'' She glanced at the ring, then slipped it on her finger. She was right, he was a man with his own agenda. Fortunately, it coincided with hers tonight. ''Okay then, it's only for a few hours. I appreciate it. I'm Molly McGuire.''

''Molly McGuire.''

''Don't even think it. I've heard every joke ever invented.''

Amusement showed in his eyes. ''I'm sure you have. I'm Nick Bailey.''

Before Molly could shake his offered hand, a sultry, female voice projected through the pub.

''Nicky, darling, I've been looking all over for you. One of the bellmen said he saw you come in here.''

Molly swung around and saw a voluptuous dark-haired woman saunter across the room. For a moment Molly almost wished her own short light brown hair was long and dark as the newcomer's, that she could fill out her clothes as this woman did and that she could perfect such sensuous moves by merely walking.

Most of the time she pulled her hair back so it would not get into her eyes when she painted. And she forgot to eat a lot of the time if she were involved in a project, so voluptuous curves were out.

Her musings were interrupted when she became aware the man beside her had stiffened. He stepped closer to her before greeting the newcomer.

"Carmen. When did you get back in town?" he said evenly. There was a thread of tension in his tone.

Molly didn't understand what was happening, but she could recognize things were growing tense.

"I told you I would be back, darling. And I don't have any plans to leave again for weeks." Carmen walked closer than necessary and reached up to kiss him, but he sidestepped, placing his arm across Molly's shoulders.

"Molly, I'd like to introduce Carmen Hernandez, an old friend. Carmen, I don't believe you've met Molly—my fiancée."

"Fiancée?" Carmen's sultry Latin looks flared into anger. "What the hell do you mean?" She gave Molly a disbelieving look and swung her attention back to Nick. "If anyone is getting married, it'll be you and me! What kind of game are you playing, Nicky? I don't believe this! You can't brush me off so easily. You're mine and no one else's!" Carmen's temper rose, bringing flushed color to her dusky cheeks. Her dark eyes glared at Molly. "I don't know who you think you are, but he's mine!" Contemptuously she ran her gaze over Molly. "You don't have what it takes to hold a man like Nick." Dismissing her, she turned to Nick.

"Nick—"

"Maybe you two would like to discuss this in private," Molly said, stung by yet another woman. Did she have a sign hanging around her neck saying *Insult me, I don't mind*?

Nick's hold tightened on her shoulders as if the two of them faced the world together. Nice staging, she thought, even as she wondered what she'd gotten herself into. She thought she was the one needing help. Obviously she was not the only one.

Was Nick Bailey in a similar situation as she was? How ironic, yet it would explain why he so quickly agreed to her outrageous suggestion. Molly felt she'd been thrust on stage of a play in progress—without a script.

"We broke off things weeks ago," Nick said. His reasonable tone contrasted nicely with Carmen's passionate anger, yet Molly heard the underlying steel. Molly liked a man who could be cool under fire.

"*You* said we should end things, but I'm not ready to give up on us!" Carmen said dramatically, her hand reaching out to grip his arm. "I love you. You know that. You've been cruel ignoring me, playing hard to get. I won't be pushed aside."

"Carmen, we're through. And all the drama in the world isn't going to change that. Besides, I'm engaged to another woman." He lifted Molly's left hand and let what little light came from over the bar sparkle on the diamond.

Carmen scarcely glanced at the ring. She glared instead directly at Molly. "You probably think you pulled off some kind of coup snaring Nicholas Bailey. But let me tell you, things don't end here.'' Raising her eyes to Nick, she narrowed them in anger. ''You can't get rid of me so easily, lover!''

Spinning around, she stalked from the bar, in stark contrast to her earlier sensuous entry. Molly felt as if a whirlwind had just blown through.

''That went well,'' the bartender said.

''Shut up,'' Nick responded. He released Molly and raised an eyebrow. ''Shall we head for the Zentech Reception? After Carmen's act, it should be a piece of cake.''

''At least that answers my question about why you'd agree to this cockamamie scheme. You needed me as much as I need you. More, I think. I doubt Justin's going to get so emotional when he hears we're engaged.'' Though she hoped Brittany would be put in her place! Let her believe Molly was no longer interested in rekindling the relationship with Justin because she was involved with someone even more exciting.

Nick frowned. ''She'll cool down.''

''But I doubt that's the last we'll see of her. I'd expect her at the wedding if I were you,'' Donny said. ''Her way of making sure.''

Molly looked between the two men. ''What wedding?''

''Ours, of course,'' Nick said. ''Come on, let's go see who we can shock at Zentech's party.''

CHAPTER TWO

MOLLY and Nick were alone in the elevator as it whisked them to the upper floor of the lavish hotel. Her thoughts were spinning. She would walk in with the most dynamic man there. One she was supposed to be engaged to. Would they be able to carry it off? Obviously Carmen had bought into the concept. But that had been brief, and surprising. The woman's temper had ruled. Upon closer reflection, would she realize how impossible the entire scenario was?

She glanced at Nick. He stared straight back at her, his look intimidating.

"So I have this straight—some guy dumped you for a new girlfriend and you want to appear engaged so he won't know you're upset," he said bluntly.

"I see sensitivity training plays a big part in your life," Molly murmured, annoyed at the way he put it.

"What?"

"Never mind. I guess you've nailed it. Thanks for feeding my ego. If you don't mind a suggestion or two, no one will believe we're engaged if you continue to look like you're perpetually angry. Can you smile or something? And while you're at it, could you pretend you find me captivating?"

"Captivating?"

She nodded. "I've always wanted to captivate someone. Don't you think a new fiancé would be captivated?"

''Absolutely.''

She could tell by the gleam in his eye that he was mocking her. So be it, as long as he did as she asked. She only had to get through this evening. Then she could make up something to cause a breakup in a few weeks. By then she'd be hip deep in work for the new account and would ignore Justin and Brittany. And once her coworkers caught a look at Nick, any pity for poor dumped Molly would vanish in an instant.

Amazement that Molly McGuire from the art department could attract anyone like him would more likely be in the forefront of any new gossip and speculation.

The celebration was in full swing when they reached the huge ballroom. Banners hung from the ceiling, announcing the new consortium. The mammoth floor to ceiling windows comprising two walls gave a splendid view of San Francisco, from Union Square far below, to the blue expanse of the bay, glimpsed in the distance, to the sweeping towers of the Bay Bridge.

''There you are, Molly. I wondered where you were.'' John Billings, the president of the firm greeted her. He looked at Nick with curiosity in his gaze.

''Hi John. Sorry we're late, we got held up. I'd like you to meet my fiancé, Nick Bailey.''

The die was cast. She hoped she wasn't making a huge mistake.

''Nick, good to meet you. I heard rumors our Molly was seeing someone special. You must know how proud we are of Molly and her work. She was the key component in the presentation. We wouldn't be here today without her.''

Molly flushed with surprised delight. She hadn't expected the accolade. That surprise was expanded when Nick rested his hand on the small of her back and said, "Molly is very determined—she goes after what she wants."

Molly felt a leap of sensation explode at his touch. She lost the trend of the conversation for a moment. She'd never felt so charged up from a mere touch before. What was going on? Maybe she should not have had that rum and Coke.

John moved on and others spoke to her as they moved through the room. Congratulations on her design work were called. Greetings were exchanged, questions fielded about Nick as she introduced him to everyone.

Suddenly a pathway cleared and Justin and Brittany appeared. The group around Molly quieted, eagerly watching.

"Molly, good to see you. We were wondering where you were," Justin said. "Get tied up with last minute work?"

"Why, hello, Molly. We were beginning to wonder if you were going to show up or not," Brittany said, clinging to Justin as if he were a life preserver and she in danger of drowning. The tall blonde was model slim and flawless. The ice blue dress clung to a thin figure that showed it to perfection.

She dressed up well, Molly had to give her that. Normally she wore jeans and work shirts like the rest of the art department.

But for once, Molly didn't care about Brittany. Or Justin. She was savoring her moment of triumph.

Nick stepped forward and offered his hand.

"Blame me for keeping Molly. Nick Bailey. Are you someone who works for Molly?"

Justin's startled look was priceless. He frowned, shook Nick's hand and shook his head. "I don't work for Molly. We work together sometimes on projects. I'm Justin Morris, an account executive for Zentech." He looked at Molly. "I didn't know you'd be coming with anyone."

"Really?" Molly said, smiling up at Nick, startled to see the warmth in his own gaze as he met her eyes, his arm coming around her shoulders again. "Now why would you think that?" she asked, refraining from looking at Brittany.

"It's hard to share Molly," Nick said. "But this event is important to her, so we came. Better late than never." He glanced at Brittany, dismissing her with carelessness, returning his attention to Molly.

Molly almost laughed aloud at Brittany's stunned expression. With her good looks, she rarely had men pass her over with hardly a glance.

Molly looked at Justin and felt a sudden pang. She'd wasted several weeks of her life mourning the end of their dating. And now, nothing. Was she so fickle? Or had she only been in love with the notion of being a part of a couple? Had the glamour of being sought after, wined and dined in fashionable restaurants gone to her head?

Whatever, she was relieved to no longer be under his spell. She felt gloriously free. She no longer had anything to prove to Justin Morris or Brittany Taylor!

"We have to move on, Nick already met John. Now I want him to meet some of our new Japanese partners," Molly said.

"Is that your engagement ring?" Brittany asked, staring at Molly's hand. Her tone implied she could hardly believe Molly could ever get engaged.

Molly showed off her grandmother's ring. It was lovely, if set in an old-fashioned style.

Just then a photographer snapped a couple of pictures, the sudden flash startling.

Brittany preened, leaning forward a bit, smiling at the man.

Molly stepped back, pushing against Nick. She looked up at him and smiled. "Shall we mingle some more?"

He leaned forward until he was just a whisper away.

"Is this captivating enough for you?"

"You're doing great. I really appreciate it," she said in a low voice for his ears alone.

Another flash exploded.

Looking around, Molly frowned. "You'd think in this day and age they could take photos without being so intrusive."

"It's an important event for the company," Justin said. "I'm sure they want to record it for the annual report." He, too, had turned toward the photographer, smiling genially.

Molly was content to let Justin and Brittany claim the limelight. She was ready to leave. Mission accomplished.

"If you'll excuse us," Molly said, stepping away.

Nick left his hand on her shoulder as they walked through the crowd.

"That's all I could have asked," she said with satisfaction. "Thanks."

"The encounter with Justin and Brittany—is that the sole reason for the big deception?"

"Brittany, mostly. I can't stand her. We've both worked at Zentech for almost seven years, and it doesn't get easier."

"She's a self-centered woman on the make."

Molly glanced up. "Most men find her fascinating."

"Most men find her body fascinating, there's a difference," he said firmly.

"I'm not sure I see the difference."

"Maybe you have to be a guy. So tell me Molly McGuire, what do you do for Zentech? Your president thinks highly of you."

"I've worked there since I graduated from the art school. I'm one of the art directors now. Recently I got lucky in getting assigned on the project for the Hamakomoto account."

"Lucky? Or talented?"

She grinned. "I like your thinking. Mostly I direct layouts, or full spectrum designs for our clients, such as corporate literature, stationery, ad designs, Web sites, you name it, if it's art involved, my team can do it!"

"And how does Justin play into all this?"

"He's a guy I dated for a while. If Brittany wasn't so awful, our breaking up wouldn't have been such a big deal. But she's a real witch. And I'm tired of her patronizing attitude." She glanced over her shoulder and saw the woman in conversation with the photographer—probably arranging another picture that would show Brittany to best advantage. "Justin is one of the account executives at Zentech, so we're always thrown together. Mostly I wanted to save face before the rest of the crew. It's hard not to feel like I'm constantly the object of pity when walking through the offices."

"So mission accomplished. Then we're finished here?"

She nodded. "As soon as we speak to our clients. Are you in a hurry to leave?"

He shook his head. "Your encounter was milder than ours with Carmen."

Molly smiled, nodding to another guest. "If Justin had been Latin, do you think he'd have thrown a scene?"

Nick looked over the crowd and spotted Justin. "Not unless it served his needs."

"He is focused on the main chance—for his advancement. But aren't all corporate types?"

"Are we?" Nick asked.

"You tell me."

"Maybe you're right."

Despite her earlier misgivings, Molly realized she was enjoying the reception. She felt a twinge of guilt every time she introduced Nick as her fiancé, but squelched it knowing most of the people she talked to didn't know her except as a business contact. She'd arrange to have the breakup known in a couple of weeks and move on.

It was close to eight when the event wound down.

Molly and Nick began to move toward the elevator. She couldn't complain about his attention, it had been focused on her the entire time. Actually, it was quite heady. If she ever captivated anyone, she hoped he'd act as Nick had all evening.

The elevator was crowded on the ride down, so conversation was limited. Walking through the lobby a short time later, Molly felt a hint of regret that the evening was coming to an end.

"Thanks again, Nick. I appreciate all you've done."

"The help was mutual. Donny knew Carmen would prove troublesome."

"And you didn't suspect?"

"We were through a couple of months ago. And she knows it. But I heard she was coming in today. I thought having the confrontation in the bar at that time of day would make it easier than somewhere more public. I was not about to meet with her in private. Never trust a woman scorned."

"Succinct advice. I'll remember that. She seems like the type who loves creating a scene."

"She is dramatic. Like your Brittany."

"Please, Brittany isn't mine. And if I never see her again, it would be too soon!" But she would be at Zentech the next morning, as she had for the entire time Molly had worked there. Oh well, some things must be endured. At least Molly had lost the pity of her fellow workers. Most had been delighted to meet Nick, and seemed happy for her. She'd intercepted more than one interested gaze directed at her escort. Her stock had shot up.

He escorted her out to the sidewalk. The fog was drifting in, dropping the temperature rapidly. Tourists still wandered along the sidewalk. The clang of the cable cars could be heard as they lumbered up Powell Street.

''Do you have a car?'' Nick asked. ''Or need a ride home?''

''No, I came in a cab. I'll get one and be home in no time.''

He nodded to the doorman and in seconds a cab slid to the curb.

''Thanks again, Nick, for helping me out.'' She held out her hand.

''I'm sure a fiancé gets some perks,'' he said, ignoring her hand and sweeping her into his arms to give her a quick kiss.

Another flash—from a camera, or from the excitement of his kiss? Molly wasn't sure. Several hours of chitchat and she knew little about the man. She had not expected a kiss—nor to feel like she did receiving it.

Then she was bundled into the cab. ''Goodbye, Molly McGuire.''

''Wow,'' she said softly, looking over her shoulder out the back window as the cab pulled away. Justin wasn't the one she should lament losing. But Nick Bailey might be.

CHAPTER THREE

NICK BAILEY stared at the lifestyle section of the paper his PA placed on his desk the next morning with frustrated anger. Damn, he should have suspected last night. Why hadn't he? Just because he'd been playing a role didn't mean others didn't take it seriously. Or that he should have let his defenses down. Now he needed to do damage control before things got out of hand.

"Something you wanted to share, boss?" Helen asked. The fifty-five year old woman had been with Nick since he'd taken over the reins of Magellan's Hotels ten years earlier. The chain of luxury hotels covered the west coast, from San Diego to Seattle. The flagship hotel was the first, San Francisco's gem. He made it his headquarters as his father had prior to his death a decade ago.

The black and white newspaper photos he stared at were a surprise. Why hadn't he considered the newspapers when cameras were flashing last night? Molly had mentioned recording the event for posterity—he knew the company had had a number of roaming photographers. But so, apparently, had the local newspaper.

Eyeing the photos, a feeling of disquiet pervaded. Had it been a setup—some sort of con? Play up the engaged feature, then hold him up for some kind of extortion? Or had she been merely trying to align herself with him, hoping for some kind of gain? A lot of advancement came from connections. And Nick had had women after him since he'd started in the business world—wanting a share of the money or glamour running the hotels brought.

But he had not expected this.

He and Molly were headline news on the lifestyle section. *Notorious Marriage—Shy Hotel Guru Nick Bailey Landed at Last?*

He was sure Donny had never anticipated such a turn when he suggested Nick play fiancé to a stranger.

The idea had held merit when he'd considered Carmen and her increasing demands. He'd tried to break things off gently. Then not so gently. But she didn't seem to get that they were through.

Would the confrontation last night confirm it for her?

How ironic if the newspaper article sealed their ending, yet opened a can of worms with Molly McGuire. He felt a twinge of disappointment at the thought Molly would be contacting him soon with some suggestion or demand.

Helen stood by the desk, studying the splashy pictures, leaning closer to scan the article.

"I haven't sent her flowers or arranged a reservation at any of your usual restaurants," she murmured.

"It's not what you think," he replied, folding the paper and tossing it to the corner of the desk. He'd get Donny to check it out. Find out just who Molly McGuire was, what she was after, and nip anything she had in mind in the bud. He hadn't reached the success he enjoyed by being passive!

"I think an engagement means you are planning to

marry the woman. What's not to think?'' Helen asked.

''The reporter got it wrong. We're not engaged.''

''One picture has a ring flashing.''

''Do you have the figures from the Portland site?''

''Changing the subject, boss?'' Helen walked back to her office and began to look through the folders and reports that were stacked on her desk.

When the phone rang, she grabbed it without breaking stride.

Glancing up, she smiled. ''Donny's on line one,'' she called.

Nick snatched the phone. ''You and your dumb ideas.''

''Seen the paper, huh?''

''I never considered the media would be there. Maybe Molly arranged it. Ever consider a breach-of-promise suit? What with palimony awards going like gangbusters, maybe she thought to cash in on something like it. How much do we know about her?''

''Hey, she seemed nice enough. Want me to run a check on her?''

''Yes. Let me know once you find out something.''

''You're lucky you didn't land on a spot on Channel 8 news. The kiss was a nice touch.''

''What kiss?'' Nick knew full well what kiss. How had Donny known?

''Didn't you see page two?''

Nick reached for the paper, flipped it open to page two, where the article continued. There was a photo of his goodbye kiss. One impulse after months of grinding work, and it's captured for the world. Damn.

"So are you going to see her again?" Donny asked.

"No. It was for one night only, remember? Hell, you arranged it. But I don't like loose ends, and this article doesn't ring true. Find out why it's in the paper and see what we can do for damage control. And find out what Molly's game is."

"Hey, cuz, I live to serve. But don't you have a publicity department that could put a better spin on it?"

"And have anyone else know the full situation? Not damn likely. You're it."

"And Carmen?"

"She got the message yesterday."

"Until the first time she sees you someplace without fiancée in tow. If she suspects trouble in paradise, she'll move back in for the kill."

"Charming. I'll worry about that when it comes. Have you turned up anything yet on that other matter?"

"Give me a break, Nick, I just started a couple of days ago. These things take time. I have to make friends before anyone confides in me. If I push, they'll clam up forever."

Donny Morgan had opened a private investigative agency several years back, after ten years with the Los Angeles Police Department.

Nick had hired his cousin in an attempt to discover if there was embezzlement from the bar. Sales figures had fallen recently, yet any time Nick glanced in, the place seemed to be doing great. He had suspicions but needed proof before proceeding. Donny had agreed to go undercover to find the proof.

"How's Aunt Ellen?" Donny asked.

"About the same." Another worry. His mother's failing health had caused concern for several weeks. The nurse who watched her full time was always optimistic, but the doctor seemed more reserved.

Nick hated the helpless feeling he had around his mother. He wanted her to get well, resume her normal activities. Return to the vibrant woman she'd once been.

"Give her my love the next time you see her. Gotta go."

Helen dropped off the folder he wanted, and took the newspaper, studying the new photo as she walked back to her desk.

Nick focused his attention on the report, doing his best to push Miss Molly McGuire from his mind. If she thought to make anything of last night, she'd soon know better. They had an agreement for one night. That was all. End of story.

But he wondered what she was doing at that moment—plotting and planning?

Molly worked straight through lunch. She'd arrived early at the office to catch up on several projects pushed to a back burner when working on the Hamakomoto account. Now that the Hamakomoto deal was signed and sealed, she had other assignments that needed her attention. The bulk of her duties over the foreseeable future would be overseeing the Hamakomoto line, but she still had a couple of accounts that were favorites. She'd delegate others when the workload grew to be too much.

But that would be in the future. More immediately,

she planned to treat herself to a pampered weekend at a spa in the wine country—starting tomorrow. The long hours leading up to the final agreement with the Japanese firm had put a dent in her leisure time. She was taking off early Friday afternoon and wouldn't return to the city until Monday morning. She could hardly wait!

She reached for another portfolio, enjoying the sense of accomplishment that accompanied clearing up loose ends. She spread the sketches on the wide drawing table, hitched her chair closer and reached for her charcoal. She wanted to finish the last drawing before taking a break.

The murmur through the wide-open space the artists use stopped. Molly glanced up—right into the dark eyes of Nick Bailey.

She stared at him, surprised to see him. Hadn't they said goodbye forever?

Instantly she remembered flirting and playing the role of devoted fiancée last night. He didn't look like he was ready to flirt today.

The dark suit and pristine white shirt he wore emphasized his rugged masculine looks. He carried himself with a confidence that insured he would never go unnoticed. Just standing there, he seemed to fill the space. Funny, she'd never thought the large open room particularly small before.

He glanced at the other artists, who all quickly became involved with their work, except for Brittany. She was across the floor, separated from them by a dozen workstations, but she stared across the room at Nick and Molly.

If Nick noticed, he ignored it. He looked directly

at Molly. ''We need to talk.'' That steel beneath his easygoing tone surfaced. Just as it had with Carmen.

''About what?'' She regarded him warily. What was he doing here? How had he tracked her down? Of course, he'd known she worked for Zentech. How hard was it to show up at the front desk and ask for her?

But why had the receptionist let him come back unescorted? That was not standard operating procedure.

''Have you seen today's paper?'' he asked.

She shook her head. ''I don't read the local newspaper that often. Why?''

He paced behind her desk to the bank of windows. She had a prime workstation—right next to the wall of windows which provided a lot of natural light. One day Molly wanted to have a corner office with windows on two walls, but for now this was all she could get. At Zentech, offices were for account executives, not art directors.

He turned and slid his hands into the trouser pockets, studying her with that familiar frown.

Molly refrained from fidgeting, but it took a lot of willpower. She glanced around the room quickly, noting how everyone appeared to be working. But she knew they were listening avidly. At least Brittany was too far away to hear anything. Molly refused to give more fodder to the gossip mill.

''Come with me,'' she said, hopping down from her high stool and heading for the exit sign. The only place to have privacy would be the stairwell. Pushing open the fire door, she checked to make sure they were alone before turning to face Nick.

"What is it you want? I must say I didn't expect to see you again."

"Didn't you? I find that hard to believe. Especially after the press coverage at last night's event."

"The press? I knew they would be there. Our new account is big news. The plans we have impact several San Francisco firms as well as satellite locations around the globe. Did someone try to interview you?" Not possible, Nick had been by her side all evening. Unless it had been after she left.

"There are photos of us in today's paper—complete with story about our whirlwind romance and engagement."

Molly stared dumbfounded. "What? I didn't give them any story. I didn't even talk to a reporter. You were with me the entire time, you know I didn't." How had the paper picked up on the engagement story and why? The coverage should have focused on the new contract. "Though I guess we weren't exactly making a secret of our supposed engagement. I mean, that was the whole reason we went there together, remember?"

"It doesn't matter much who gave it to the reporter. The fact is it's in today's paper and has probably been read by everyone."

"So it'll blow over in a day or two. I mean, who cares if an art director from Zentech gets engaged?"

"The entire social and financial sector of San Francisco does when her fiancé is Nicholas Bailey of Magellan Hotels."

Molly's knees went weak. She plopped down on a step staring at Nick. Running her suddenly damp palms against her jeans, she shook her head. "Impossible. You can't be the head of Magellan Hotels. They've been around for decades and are family owned.''

''Founded by my grandfather right after the war. Taken over by me when my father died ten years ago.''

''What were you doing hanging around a bar in the middle of the afternoon?'' she asked. ''I thought you—'' She stopped abruptly.

Resting a foot on the step beside her, he leaned closer, resting his forearm on his raised knee. ''You thought what?''

''Never mind. Sheesh, I never made the connection. And when people asked you what you did last night, you never said you owned the hotel! You just said you were in the service industry.''

''Which hotels are. But Zentech wasn't my company, I wasn't going to take away the limelight from your special evening.''

''So what do you want—for me to send a retraction to the paper?'' Molly couldn't believe it. The head of Magellan Hotels had agreed to act as a temporary fiancé? It didn't make sense.

''Did you give them the story?'' he asked.

Molly shook her head.

''Then it's unlikely they'd take a retraction from you. And after the photographs they published, I doubt anyone would believe it anyway. Besides, it's gone beyond that. My mother saw the article, and the pictures, thanks to her busybody nurse.''

''And she doesn't approve?'' Molly could understand that. She'd want to meet a proposed fiancée of any son she'd ever have before he popped the question. "Tell her the truth. I'm sure she doesn't move in the same circles Brittany and Justin do, so her knowing won't blow my cover. Anyway, I plan for us to break up soon."

"How?"

She shrugged. "I'll go to a few events alone and if anyone asks, I'll just say it didn't work."

Nick hesitated. "Not yet."

"What do you mean, not yet. Of course I wouldn't do it the very next day after telling everyone. But soon. Before it goes on too long."

"You'll have to hold off."

"What? Why?"

"My mother's been in failing health for some time. This article has changed her attitude completely. Her nurse and doctor think it's just the thing to get her back on her feet. She's shown more improvement since reading the article than she has in weeks."

"What's wrong with her?"

"She had pneumonia last winter, and never completely shook its effects. She's lost weight, lost interest in everything."

Molly drummed her fingers on her thigh. "Okay, then we don't do a retraction."

"There's more. She wants to meet my fiancée."

"Tell her we broke up."

"I just told you, she's changed completely because she thinks I'm getting married. She wants to meet my future bride. She wants input into the wedding. She's showing an interest in something for the first time in months. If you think I'm going to kill that, you're crazy."

"But we aren't engaged," Molly protested.

"You know that and I know that. And Donny knows. But to the rest of the world we are. Didn't you introduce me as your fiancé to everyone at the Zentech affair last night? I bet I could call a dozen in this morning to confirm it."

"It was just for the night." She was beginning to suspect where he was going with this.

"I helped you out, now it's your turn to help me out."

"I did, with Carmen."

"I did with Justin *and* Brittany. That's two to your one. You still owe me."

Outraged, Molly jumped to her feet. "I do not owe you anything." He rose and they stood staring at each other, on the same level since Molly was standing a step above the landing. She noticed the hard look around his eyes, the determination in every nuance. The slight hint of aggression.

"Then you won't mind if I stop by Justin's office on my way out and let him know the whole thing was a sham? Or maybe let Brittany know we were just fooling?"

"You wouldn't."

"Try me," he urged softly.

"Why would you want people you know to believe you're engaged to me? I'm a daydreaming artist who wears jeans and cross-trainers. If you are who you say you are, you're rich. You probably have dozens of women falling at your feet. Who would believe we are engaged?"

"Interesting slant, don't you think? But the fact is the newspaper reported it, complete with captivating photographs. Anyone who sees them will believe it."

"I think you're nuts. How do I know any of this is even true?"

"Do you think I'd make it up?" His eyes gleamed dangerously. "Get a newspaper."

Molly tried to think of options. How could a silly, harmless deception turn out to become such a big deal? Which would become even more compounded if she perpetuated it.

"What do you want me to do?" she asked suspiciously.

"Come tonight to meet my mother. We'll have dinner at her home. I can't guarantee she'll join us for the meal, but she'll at least get to meet you. Pretend we are engaged. Once she's better, we can tell her we didn't suit and break it off. But not until she is well again! This is the first encouraging sign we've had. I'm not going to jeopardize it!"

"How do I know you are really the head of Magellan Hotels?" Did he think she just waltzed off with complete strangers?

"Come back to the hotel if you like. I'll show you my office, let you meet my secretary who will vouch for me. She worked for my father before me—has known me since I was a kid," he said. He stepped closer, crowding Molly's space. She took a step backward until she was up against the wall.

"There are a dozen people the other side of that door," she warned. It was a foolish bluff. He wasn't really threatening her. But he was taking up all the air. She gazed at him, reminded again of pirates plundering and taking what they wanted.

"I'll have Donny join us tonight, if you'll feel more comfortable."

"Donny?" She needed more room. Slowly she eased to her right, away from Nick. He didn't push the issue. His intimidation technique worked great. She wondered if she could try it sometime.

"My cousin, the bartender."

"Your cousin tends bar? And you expect me to believe you're the head of Magellan Hotels?"

"He's a private investigator working on a case. Don't tell anyone. And since he got me into this mess, I figure he can be there to help us out of it."

"You could have said no."

"And had no defense against Carmen?"

Molly shook her head. "Don't try that on me. You don't need any help against Carmen or any other woman."

"But I do need your help with my mother. We've tried every treatment the doctor suggested. This is the first thing that has given me hope."

She stared at him, hearing the sincerity in his tone. He had helped her out last night. How hard would it be to pretend for another evening? She sighed.

"Okay, give me the address and I'll show up at seven. One night only. Then we're even."

"Not acceptable. I need you to play along until she is better. Then we can stage a fight, break up and go our separate ways."

"And just how long to you expect that to be?" Molly asked wondering if she'd taken a fall down the White Rabbit's burrow?

"As long as it takes. A few weeks, a month or two at the most."

"A month or two? I can't put my life on hold for

a month or two! You're asking me to disrupt my entire life for you. And I don't even know you."

"I figured we'd come down to this. How much?"

She stared at him. Then glanced down at her chest. She didn't see the sign but she knew it was there.

"Do you lie in bed nights thinking up ways to be insulting?" she asked, moving to the door, throbbing with the unfairness of it all. She'd never asked for any of this.

"I have better things to do in bed."

Immediately images of him and Carmen sprang to mind. She didn't want to think about that.

"Well then your talents must come naturally. I'm not asking for a thing from you! And I'm backing out of tonight." She threw open the door. "Find a way to tell your mother the truth."

"The truth?" Justin asked, standing near the door in the open work area. "What truth?"

Molly wanted to jump back into the stairwell and slam the door. Was she living under bad karma or something? What was Justin doing here? She was caught.

Nick stepped into the breach. "My mother wants us to have a huge, lavish wedding. Molly wants something quiet and intimate, but she hates to hurt my mother's feelings," he said smoothly.

"Was there something you wanted?" Molly asked Justin. Of course no one asked her what she wanted—which was to be left alone and not have ex-boyfriends and current fiancés glaring at each other with that macho display men had when fighting over a woman. Puh-lease, it was too much! Especially since Justin didn't care a fig about her, and Nick only wanted a pretend arrangement.

"I need Nathan to mock up a layout for me, but he said he's working on something else for you and you'd have to okay being bumped. It won't take him long. You're always ahead of schedule, it won't delay your deadline. Help me out here, Molly," Justin said.

Molly glared at him, knowing she was taking out her frustration on the man, but it was so like him. Suddenly she realized how often he had charmed things from her when they'd been dating. Had that been the reason he'd been so attentive?

"Go ask Brittany. See if she has someone who can help you out."

"She doesn't."

"Then wait your turn. Next time schedule better." She turned back to Nick. He was leaning casually against the doorjamb, as if he didn't have a care in the world. Only the tightness around his eyes belied his pose.

"I have things to do, even if you don't," she snapped.

"I'll pick you up after work. We aren't finished our discussion."

Conscious of the eyes and ears of the others, Molly knew she was trapped. She nodded, but she wasn't happy about the situation. "I get off at five. But I'll have to change clothes. I can meet you there." Then it struck her—she didn't know where he lived. And a fiancée should know that, shouldn't she? But she couldn't ask with Justin hovering over her.

As if he could read minds, Nick shook his head. "You know I don't mind taking you home and waiting while you change. See you at five, darling.'' Leaning over, he kissed her again, drawing it out beyond a mere brush of lips.

Molly almost exploded. She didn't want a kiss. She didn't want anything from the man. But, conscious of Justin, of Brittany and half a floor of coworkers, she made no fuss. Her blood was pounding when Nick pulled back and winked, which drove her crazy! She watched him leave then glanced at Justin who still stood smoldering next to her.

''When did you meet him?'' he asked.

''After we stopped dating. I've got work to do.'' She stalked to her drafting table and hitched herself up on the high stool. Picking up the charcoal, she couldn't believe all that had happened in the few moments since she'd first picked up the pencil.

''I need Nathan,'' Justin said. He'd followed her to her drafting table and acted as if he was planted there until he got the response he wanted.

''What part of no do you not understand?'' she said. Her temper was growing shorter by the second. If he had a lick of sense, he'd detect it and leave her alone.

''Hey, what's got you upset? It's an easy favor. You always helped me in the past. We're still friends, Molly, right?'' He moved closer, as if to charm her into getting his way.

Molly could just imagine the gossip that would run rampant that afternoon. She kept her head down, eyes on her paper.

''No, we are not friends. No, I will not bump Nathan's current workload. Go charm Brittany.

Surely she'd give you what you want, you two being so tight and all.''

''Jealous?'' he asked softly.

''Hardly,'' she scoffed. ''Our breaking up was the best thing to happen to me. I met Nick and look where I am now.''

Right between a rock and a hard place, but Justin didn't know that.

Finally realizing she meant what she said, he left, grumbling the entire time. Molly tried to pick up where she'd left off. But images of Nick danced in her mind. He would drive her totally insane if she continued to have anything to do with him. He had no business kissing her in full sight of the entire art staff. Heat washed through her as she remembered her reaction. He was certainly an expert. But if they were even going to discuss a pretend engagement certain rules had to be established. She'd make that perfectly clear to him tonight when he picked her up.

Before or after dinner with his mother?

Was that for real? Was his mother suffering ill health? Could the news of a possible wedding have made her feel better?

Molly stared at the layout, all thoughts of work fleeing. She didn't wish anyone ill. It wasn't such a hardship to her personal life to pretend to be engaged. She hadn't exactly been burning the midnight oil with dates recently.

And much as she might like to snap her fingers at Nick Bailey and his arrogant demand, she couldn't turn her back on a sick woman.

Or was Nick Bailey playing some kind of mind game with her? He'd seemed genuinely annoyed with the newspaper spread. Which reminded her. She rang the receptionist and asked if she had a copy of the daily paper.

When a newspaper was delivered, Molly turned to the lifestyle section, reading every word of the article, studying each photograph. The poses the photographer had captured were convincing. Even she would have thought it true if she hadn't known better. And the sidebar article told her a bit about the marriage-shy hotel magnate. She quickly scanned a short list of names he'd been associated with, suspecting those women hated having their names listed as former girlfriends. Except maybe Carmen, who could be the type to like any kind of fame she could get.

Not so Molly. Yet she had no one to blame but herself for the article and the predicament she was in. If only she and Shelly hadn't concocted such a dumb idea. If only she had marched in to last night's reception alone and unentangled, and faced Justin, Brittany and the pity of her coworkers.

She reached for a telephone book and looked up the number for the Magellan Hotel on Union Square and dialed it. After a surprisingly easy screening, she was connected with Nicholas Bailey.

''Bailey.''

She'd recognize that voice anywhere.

''Just checking to make sure you are who you say you are,'' she said, and hung up.

Okay, so he probably was the head honcho of a hugely successful hotel chain. She could deal with that. What she wasn't sure about was pulling off the charade he asked. One night to save face among casually acquainted businessmen and women was quite different from days or weeks of fooling family.

How ironic. The last man she'd want to get entangled with was another corporate executive with his own agenda.

What if his mother really started planning a wedding? How cruel to snatch it away once her health improved. Wouldn't it be better to tell the truth now and give her hope he would find someone soon to fall in love with and marry?

She wondered if Nick's mother knew about Carmen. There's someone who would relish a temporary engagement. Hoping, of course, to turn it into reality. Somehow, Molly didn't see her as someone Nick or anyone else would take home to meet mother.

Promptly at five, Molly stepped outside the high-rise office building. Despite the heavy traffic and parking premiums, Nick had parked directly in front of the building.

No matter the true situation, Molly couldn't help feel a small thrill when she saw him. For a moment—just an instant—she wished they were just two people going out together with all the exploring of likes and dislikes that came with meeting a new man for the first time.

"Satisfied?" he asked, opening the door for her.

"About?"

"Who I am."

She ignored the comment and slid into the car. The leather seats felt wonderful, soft and conforming. She would love to have a car like this one. And it probably cost a mint. Welcome to the world of the rich, Molly, she thought whimsically.

"Hi there Molly McGuire," Donny said from the back seat.

She half turned to see him. The bartender/private investigator's grin was infectious as ever.

"Hi yourself. I think you should have just filled my drink order yesterday and ignored the other request."

"Ah, what a tangled web we weave... But you and Nick are naturals. He helped you out, you helped him out. Works for me."

Nick slid in behind the wheel and started the engine.

"I spoke with Mrs. Braum before I left work. She's my mother's nurse. Mother is looking forward to meeting you. We'll stop by your place so you can change and then head for home."

Molly became immediately defensive. Her job didn't exactly go with designer suits and pristine white shirts. She had charcoal smudged on one thigh. A dusting of chalk along the left leg and on the arm of her shirt.

She didn't work in some pristine office setting, but with materials that spilled, smeared, and crumbled. She hadn't wanted to meet his mother dressed this way, thus her earlier request to change clothes. He could at least give her credit for that.

Nick pulled into traffic and soon made the turn onto the Embarcadero.

"Don't you need directions?" Molly asked. He was heading for her apartment building, but how had he known?

"I know the way."

"How do you know where I live?"

"Donny told me."

She looked over her shoulder into the back seat. "And how do you know?"

He grinned unrepentantly. "I know all. You two had better spend the next few minutes or so going over your backgrounds, so you don't mess up when you meet Aunt Ellen," Donny suggested. "I've given Nick the high points about you, and drew up a quick page about him," he continued, sliding a sheet of paper over the seat back.

Molly took it and began to read. Vital statistics, age, birth date, where he attended school.

"What do you mean, you gave the high points of my life to Nick? Did you investigate me?" She turned and glared at Donny.

"Hey, I thought we were keeping me undercover," Donny said to Nick.

"Like we could do that with you saying you'd given me the high points in her life. Anyway, she knows about your assignment."

"It's supposed to be a secret," Donny complained. "Need to know, and all that."

"Except for family," Molly murmured. "How close can a fiancée get? Just think of me as your new cousin-to-be. So I'm to memorize all this before dinner? Did Nick get a crash course, too?"

"You're an only child, though your mother is one of five siblings, who all had children, so you have lots of cousins," he began to recite. "Your parents live in Fremont, where you grew up. Currently they are on a once-in-a-lifetime cruise, courtesy of your father's company for a banner year in sales. Your mother teaches at the School for the Deaf. You excelled in high school, and were an honors student at the School for the Arts. You've lived for six years in a renovated loft flat near China Basin. You appear to have lots of friends, but,'' he flicked her another look, ''few serious boyfriends.''

''You could have asked me, I would have told you what you need to know.'' Molly was ruffled he'd had Donny investigate her. Maybe she should hire someone to investigate him, see how he liked it.

''I still need to know your favorite colors, foods, kind of movies you like, and books, that kind of thing,'' Nick said.

''Couldn't get all that in the few hours I had to work,'' Donny apologized.

''I need to know that about you, too.'' Was she going along with this? What happened to putting her foot down and insisting on ground rules? Granted he helped her out of a sticky situation yesterday and today with Justin. But he couldn't call all the shots. She was putting herself out for him and wasn't even sure she liked him.

Nick smoothly maneuvered the car through the traffic, even as he began to respond, ''My favorite color is blue, favorite food southern fried chicken—even though I know it's supposed to be bad to eat fried foods. I like action adventure movies, when I get a chance to rent them. I rarely see them at the theater. I have season tickets for the 49ers and the symphony. I like Mozart. Don't read much, but when I do it's mysteries. What about you?''

Okay, so maybe he wasn't just a man with an agenda. ''I like blue, too. My favorite food is chocolate. I think it should be listed as one of the basic food groups. Comedies are my thing—books and movies. And sometimes a really good romance. I do not care a thing about football. I do like music of all kinds, however.''

''I now pronounce you man and fiancée,'' Donny said from the back.

''Shut up,'' Nick and Molly said in unison.

''Have you thought of a reason your mother hasn't heard of me before seeing the newspaper this morning?'' Molly asked. ''I mean, isn't that odd? Or are the two of you not close?''

''We are as close as most, I suppose. And the reason I kept you away was because of her poor health, of course. I sheltered her from a lot, I don't think she'll suspect anything is wrong.''

''And, it's been such a whirlwind affair anyway, right?'' Molly said.

''What do you mean?''

''Didn't you read the article in the paper? Did you only look at the pictures? According to a reliable source, whom I suspect was that witch Brittany, it was a whirlwind romance. It would have to be, since I was seeing Justin until recently. And we all know about Carmen.''

''I sure hope Aunt Ellen doesn't know about Carmen,'' Donny said. ''Or you're toast, my friend.''

Nick stopped before an older, six storied apartment building. He double parked, then looked at her. ''We'll wait here.''

''Fine. I'll make it quick.'' Molly opened the door and hurried inside, grateful for a few minutes to herself. Maybe she should just lock her door and never leave again.

Yet, while she wasn't sure it was wise to get involved in the scheme, she was curious about Nick. Where he had grown up. What his mother was like. Chances were good that none of them had anything in common and after tonight, no one would suspect a thing wrong when they broke off the engagement.

Once again in the luxurious car twenty minutes later, Molly watched as Nick drove competently in the rush-hour traffic, up California Street's steep hill and into Pacific Heights. In only seconds, he turned on a cross street and before long pulled into a driveway on Washington Street and stopped by a lovely old home. The Tudor architecture was softened by the bougainvillea that grew along the corners of the house and the lovely mock orange shrubs with their fragrant blossoms.

"Is this where you live?" Molly asked. Some of the homes were close to a hundred years old, built shortly after the great earthquake and fire. They were large, beautifully constructed, and costly.

"My mother does. I live in an apartment on Nob Hill. A word of warning, Molly. I do not want my mother upset. She's in frail health and I will do anything I need to for her to get better. Are we agreed on this? No discussion about anything controversial, got it?"

"Gee, this is a match made in heaven. Threats, insults, investigations and more threats. What more could a woman ask?" she said.

Donny got out and opened the door for Molly. "Show time. Did you memorize the facts I gave you?"

"I haven't even finished reading them. I know—

I'll slip into the bathroom, commit everything to memory then tear the paper into tiny bits and flush away the evidence.''

''It could be worse, she could be without a sense of humor,'' he said over the top of the car to his cousin.

Nick scowled and held out his hand. Reluctantly, Molly walked around and put hers into his, feeling his fingers close over hers. Someone should curb his autocratic tendencies, she thought. Turning to face the house, she hoped they could pull off their crazy charade for the sake of a sick woman. But she had a bad feeling about it.

CHAPTER FOUR

NICK led Molly into a formal living room before excusing himself to check on his mother. Molly suddenly wished she'd had a bit of time with Nick to fine tune their story. It was one thing to bluff their way through a casual business reception—but something else again to converse with a family member at great length.

Molly gazed around the room, fascinated despite her worry. It was elegant, fashionably furnished with a blend of antiques and modern pieces. A little cool and sterile, to her mind. She liked more color, some clutter.

''Nick was raised here?'' she asked Donny.

Donny nodded looking around as if following her thoughts. ''And scared his mother half to death all the time he was growing up that he'd destroy something valuable. It was bad enough for the rest of us when we came to visit, don't touch this, don't sit on that. I don't know how he stood living here. There is a family room in the back, where the TV is and all. He spent most of his time there. Aunt Ellen was too worried about her Ming vase, or the brocade on that old chair to give either of us free rein in this part of the house.''

Since the old chair looked as if it belonged to a museum, Molly understood Ellen Bailey's concern.

She wondered if Nick had been a rough and tumble

little boy. Had he run through the house yelling and playing, or saved his roughhousing for outside? Had he played football in high school? He had the build for it. She began to read the paper Donny had prepared, maybe she'd find the answer there.

Nick entered a few minutes later. She looked up, could quote facts and figures, but she didn't know the man at all.

"I don't think this is such a good idea," she said.

"If it was a good idea last night, it's a good idea tonight."

"Last night was different."

"How?"

"It wasn't family I was trying to fool." She waved the paper Donny had given her. "Am I really supposed to memorize all this stuff?"

"It's not like it's a lot. I'm only thirty-six."

"You went to college at Stanford, have a masters degree in business. You like to travel—you've been to a couple of places I haven't even heard of."

"And your point is?"

"We don't suit at all. Your mother will spot that in a New York minute."

"We'll soon find out. If you do your part well, she won't. She already believes the story, she's not looking to analyze anything." He took Molly's arm gently. "Come on, she's awake and anxious to meet you." Looking at his cousin, he said, "We'll be down soon."

"Don't hurry on my account. I think I'll check in the kitchen and see what's cooking."

"When Mom called to invite us, she said Shu-Wen would have dinner at seven. It'll be ready soon."

"You are not listening to me," Molly complained as they climbed the wide stairs. "We don't know enough about each other to fool anyone."

When they reached the top, Nick caught her in his arms. "I'm listening. I'm ignoring what you have to say. We will make this work. Too much depends on it."

"But—" She'd scarcely opened her mouth to protest when Nick covered her lips with his, successfully stopping any argument Molly might have voiced.

She stood in his embrace, quickly feeling her defenses melt as his kiss went on and on. His lips were warm and firm, and expert at drawing a response. His scent filled her senses and the heat they generated would have warmed a small house! He was a master and she felt like a novice. She'd had boyfriends before, but none who kissed like this. No wonder Carmen hadn't wanted to give him up.

Endless time later he pulled back and looked at her, satisfaction reflected in his gaze.

"Now you looked kissed."

"And the point is?" she asked, gazing into those dark eyes that seemed to hide so much. Her heart tripped at double time, her breathing didn't approach normal and her body heat had to register in the triple digits. How was she supposed to think coherently?

"I want my mother to believe this engagement. I'll act captivated, as long as you act adoring."

"Umm, adoring, huh? Okay, I'll give it my best shot." Bemused, Molly would have promised almost anything.

When they stepped into the large bedroom the first thing to catch Molly's eye was the hospital bed jutting from the far wall. It seemed to dominate the room. A nurse rose and smiled, walking toward them.

"I'll leave you with Mrs. Bailey. Call when you wish me to return," she said, passing to leave the room.

"Mother, I'd like you to meet Molly. Molly, my mother, Ellen Bailey," Nick said as they crossed to the bed.

The woman lying there looked almost too frail to sit up. The bed had been raised to a semi sitting position and she was propped against pillows. Painfully thin, her skin had the look of old parchment.

Her eyes held curiosity, but her smile was welcoming.

"It's nice to meet you, Molly McGuire. I wish I could say I've heard about you, but Nick kept me in the dark."

"I'm delighted to meet you, Mrs. Bailey."

"Call me Ellen, my dear. As for you, young man," she said to Nick, "We will have a talk later about keeping something this momentous a secret."

Nick walked quickly to her side and kissed her cheek. "Nothing to tell until recently. Now you know. You'll tire yourself out getting upset about it. Molly's here now and you two will have plenty of time to get to know each other once you're feeling better."

She patted the edge of the bed. "Come sit beside me, Molly and tell me all about yourself."

Molly sat gingerly on the edge, half turned toward Ellen Bailey. "There's not much to tell, I live here in the city, work at Zentech in the art department. Born and raised in California."

"As was Nick. I'm from Boston, originally. Never thought I'd want to leave when I was a girl, but Thomas Bailey swept me off my feet. Tell me how you met Nick."

Molly stared at her, while her mind spun a thousand miles an hour. Would she want to hear that they'd met at a bar? In fact, one could say Molly picked him up. The idea struck her as funny. Nick Bailey didn't seem the type to be picked up by anyone.

"I met her at a function her company held at the hotel," Nick interposed smoothly. "Was captivated from the first."

"So that's why you announced your engagement at last night's Zentech function. Full circle." Ellen nodded as if it made sense.

Molly gave a weak smile and looked at Nick. Let him field all questions, it would save wear and tear on her nerves!

"Sit down, Nick. You'll give me a crick in my neck towering over us that way," Ellen said with a frown.

Pulling a chair close, Nick sat down, close enough to Molly his leg bumped hers. She was suddenly shockingly aware of his presence and had to concentrate hard to hear what his mother was saying. If she moved her foot just a bit, she could touch him again she thought wildly. It caused her insides to quiver and she lost her train of thought. She'd been touched by men before, why did Nick's presence wreak such havoc to her nervous system?

"This is the first time you've had company in a

couple of months, I don't want you to overdo,'' he cautioned.

''Don't ever get sick, Molly, he'll worry you to death with trying to get you well instantly. I'm not going to have a setback. On the contrary, I'm feeling stronger right now than I have in a long time.'' She patted Molly's hand. ''All because I got to meet the woman Nick's planning to marry. I must confess I never thought I'd see the day. His dad and I had been married more than five years when we were his age. And Nick was already toddling around.''

Nick's narrowed gaze warned Molly to be careful, as if she needed any warning. She felt she was walking through a field of land mines.

''I bet he was a handful.'' She slanted him a glance. ''He still is.''

Ellen laughed. ''You will be good for him. Tell me about your wedding plans. You aren't going to let me read about that in the newspaper, now are you?''

Molly shook her head, her mind going blank. She was hardly used to being a fake fiancée, she had never thought about a wedding.

''Will you be married here in San Francisco or at your home church? Where are you from originally?'' Ellen asked.

Molly felt Nick's foot brush against hers in warning. Honestly, if he couldn't trust her to perpetuate the charade, why bother?

''We haven't discussed any details yet,'' she said. ''I'm from Fremont originally, so probably would want to go home to get married. Since it's only about 40 minutes away, it wouldn't be too far for friends to drive.''

"And have you set a date?"

"Not for a while," Nick said. "We want to explore being engaged first."

"We should get started on preliminary plans at least," Ellen said. "Churches and reception halls are booked months or even years in advance. In addition, Molly will need time to acquire a trousseau. And you will wish to plan a fantastic honeymoon. Will you be living in Nick's apartment, or getting something larger?"

A tiny Chinese woman appeared in the doorway, carrying a tray. "Dinner ready, Mrs. Bailey," she said as she entered. She greeted Nick, was introduced to Molly as Shu-Wen Li, the housekeeper. Mrs. Braum followed her into the bedroom.

"Need any help, Mrs. Bailey?" the nurse asked.

"In a minute. I'm still visiting," Ellen said fretfully.

"We'll let you eat, now, mother. I'm sure Shu-Wen has dinner ready for us downstairs. I'll bring Molly back to say goodnight before we leave," Nick said as he rose and held his hand out for Molly's.

She slipped it in and smiled up at him in what she hoped was an adoring pose. She was shocked by the thrill of sensation that shot through her. His hand was warm and firm. When his fingers laced through hers, her heart stuttered. This had to stop! She could scarcely think or breathe or do anything but feel the sweeping delight that pulsed through from his touch. The man was practically a stranger! Get a grip, she admonished.

Hands linked, Nick led the way downstairs. From the satisfied glimpse on his mother's face before they left, Molly knew the woman was reassured by his actions. From a distance it probably looked full of love. Ha! If she only knew.

"Shu-Wen popped in a minute ago and said dinner was ready, she just had to take your mother's tray up first," Donny said when they entered the living room. "How did things go?" He was sitting on the sofa, a drink in hand.

"Fine." Nick dropped her hand and headed for the small bar in the far corner. "Want anything?"

"Don't ask that," Donny said. "Look where that question got us yesterday."

"I'm fine," Molly said, feeling oddly bereft with the loss of Nick's touch. "Your mother is very ill, isn't she?" Nick had told her, but seeing her had reinforced his words.

"She's been sick for months," Donny said.

"She's looking better today," Nick said, turning with a small drink in hand. He sipped the amber liquid and looked at Molly. "She has some color in her cheeks and her eyes were as lively as ever. I wouldn't have thought my getting engaged would be a miracle cure for anything. But if it is, so be it." He raised his glass. "To Molly."

"Fiancée extraordinaire," Donny said, raising his glass, as well.

Molly understood Nick's worry. If his mother's thinking they were engaged would aid her recovery, Molly knew she had to keep going. She wanted the woman to recover as quickly as possible.

They could pull it off. If she deferred to him when his mother asked personal questions, it would work. All she had to do was speak as little as possible and gaze adoringly at Nick. Maybe she should try out for little theater productions when all this was over, she thought. She was getting a lot of practice in acting.

She was still bothered by the nature of their deception. Ellen Bailey seemed genuinely happy to think her son was getting married. She would feel disappointed when she discovered the truth. Molly hoped she wouldn't have a relapse.

When they moved to the dining room for dinner, Molly was pleased when the two cousins began to discuss business as they ate. She didn't mind. She could tune them out and take time to think. She glanced around the formal room. The antique furniture and heavy brocade draperies made it more elegant than anything in her parents' house. Which emphasized once again the differences in their backgrounds. She was surprised Ellen didn't think she was after Nick for his money.

"You're quiet, Molly," Nick said at one point.

She looked at him. "Nothing to say."

"A woman who doesn't speak if she has nothing to say? Snap her up, Nick!" Donny teased.

"She's already snapped up," Nick said shortly.

Donny looked at him with an odd expression. "So she is. Tell me, Molly, how did the deception go with your Zentech friends last night?"

"They seemed to believe it."

"Amazing, maybe you have a talent for acting, cuz," Donny said to Nick.

"Did you suspect I wouldn't be able to pull it off?"

Donny shrugged, his eyes alight with amusement. "And Carmen, what are you going to do with her?"

''Not a thing. She also got the message.''

''Maybe.'' Donny winked at Molly. ''Time will tell.''

When dessert had been served and coffee poured, conversation waned. A little later Nick glanced at Molly's empty cup.

''Are you finished? We can say goodbye to mother and I'll take you home.''

''I could call a cab.''

''I'll take you,'' Nick said impatiently. ''What kind of man would send his fiancée home when he could take her home himself—if only for the walk to the door?''

Molly nodded, feeling silly. Of course they had to play out the charade. Truly engaged people would love arriving at the door at the end of a date—and the kisses that would follow. She hoped he was teasing. She didn't think they needed to share any more kisses!

Ellen was dozing when they peeped in. The nurse motioned them closer. ''She made me promise to wake her. But she'll be groggy. She ate most of her dinner. It's the first time she almost completed a meal since I arrived.''

Gently she patted Ellen's shoulder. Her eyes flew open. Spying Nick and Molly, she smiled broadly. ''Did you two enjoy dinner?'' she asked struggling to sit up.

Molly could see the fatigue smudging the woman's face. ''It was delicious. I hope you feel better soon.''

''I will. I was thinking we should have an engagement party—to introduce you to all the family and friends. What do you think, Nick?''

The nurse placed several plump pillows behind her.

"It's a great idea, Mom, but we will wait until you're completely well before embarking on a party."

"Very well. But you two be thinking about it. In the meantime, I'll do my part by getting better faster than you'd ever suspect. Then we'll see about asking a few friends in so they can meet Molly!"

"Good night, Ellen," Molly said, leaning over to kiss her cheek.

"Good night, my dear. Next time you and I will spend more time together."

Once in Nick's car, Molly turned to him. "We need some guidelines for this."

"What do you mean?" he asked. Donny had elected to call a cab, so Nick and Molly were alone in the car.

"You know, what we tell people, what we do as a couple. I don't think I should get to know your mom too well, she could be upset when we part ways."

"We can hammer out the deal tomorrow evening. You'll have to stop by from time to time to see her or she'll suspect something's wrong and that would cause her undue worry which I do not want to see."

"Tomorrow evening? I won't be here, I have plans. I'm going off for the weekend."

"With a man?" The words were snapped out.

"Not that it's any of your business, but no, not with a man." Interesting reaction, she mused as he drove down one of San Francisco's steep hills. If she were involved enough with a man to go off for the weekend, she certainly wouldn't have had to ask a stranger to step in at the Zentech reception.

"Where were you going?" he asked.

"I *am* going to a spa in Napa."

He frowned. "A spa? Where you wallow around in mud and drink celery juice?" His tone was just short of horrified.

"I worked hard on the Hamakomoto account. This is my reward to myself."

"Postpone it. Donny made a good point. I can't be seen places alone now that I'm engaged or it will start rumors which could get back to my mother. I have a charity event I'm attending on Saturday, you'll have to go with me."

"I do not have to do anything! I've had this weekend planned for ages!"

"Postpone it, I'll pay for a full week there when this is over."

Molly fisted her hands and pounded her knee. "Stop trying to fix everything with money. Is that the only thing you can think of? Didn't it occur to you to just ask as a favor?"

Nick shook his head slowly. "I figured I'm asking you to postpone your weekend, the least I can do is make it up."

"Try asking and see what happens."

"Will you come with me to the fund-raiser Saturday night?" He said it through clenched teeth.

"Gee, you asked so nicely, how can I refuse?"

By the time noon rolled around on Friday, Molly had second thoughts. And thirds. Reluctant to give up on her special weekend away, she wondered what she was doing going to some charity event where she'd feel totally out of place. The chances were good

Nick's mother would never hear she hadn't gone. And she didn't figure he'd be so newsworthy there'd be more pictures in the newspaper so soon after the last spread.

Molly got a quick bite of lunch and debated taking the rest of the afternoon off. She'd asked for the time and it had been approved.

Deciding she'd rather have it later when she could go away, she set to work once she'd finished eating. Wistfully she glanced out of the windows. It was a lovely day in San Francisco. She should have gone for a walk at lunch, or eaten in the small nearby park. Maybe she'd walk home after work.

She had just sketched a preliminary mockup for a new ad program when there was a stir through the open office. She glanced up.

"Oh, oh," Molly said softly, mesmerized by the sight of Carmen Hernandez sauntering her way through the desks and drawing tables like she was on the promenade of some fashionable resort. Every man in the room had his eye on her. And quite a few of the women, but for different reasons. Once again Molly wondered what was going on at the front desk. Didn't that scatty receptionist know better than to let people wander through the offices at will?

When Carmen reached Molly's work area, she glanced around frowning. "This is where you work?" she asked. The gleam in her eye did not forebode well.

"Yes." So much for any show of civility, Molly thought, unexpectedly amused. What had Carmen expected? And how had she found her? She'd probably seen the write-up on Zentech's reception and the photographs. The whole city now knew where she could be found.

The woman shrugged in a very sexy manner, glancing around the room as if to gauge the reaction of every red-blooded male there.

Satisfied she had their attention, she looked back at Molly. "Where is your ring?" she asked, pouncing on the lack.

Molly glanced at her hand. She'd removed her grandmother's ring once the reception the other evening had ended. Scrambling for an excuse, she waved her hand around her drawing table. "It gets messy and I have to wash my hands a dozen times a day. I'm afraid I might lose it."

"If Nick gave me a diamond, I'd never take it off," Carmen declared dramatically.

"But he didn't, did he?" Molly asked cheerfully, wishing Carmen would get to the point of her visit—if there was one.

Carmen's eyes narrowed. "Not yet he hasn't. But you two aren't married, either. Where did you meet him? Does he know you work here? That you work at all? Or does he think you are as wealthy as he is? A man of his position has to worry about gold diggers."

You ought to know, Molly thought.

"Nick knows all he needs to about me." Molly rose, aware of the heightened interest of everyone within hearing distance. She glanced across the bull pen, grateful to see Brittany was not at her workstation. One blessing, but from the avid gazes of her coworkers, she knew more gossip was coming.

She'd give anything to return to her nice, quiet, placid pre-Justin life of a few months ago.

"I do not see what he finds of interest in you. We were lovers for a long time," Carmen said insolently studying Molly.

"How nice for you both."

"You aren't jealous?" Carmen asked in surprise.

"Should I be? Whatever was between you and Nick ended before I met him."

"Such passion between two people doesn't end. He's upset about something, trying to show me he is no longer interested by asking some little nobody to marry him. I can give him fire and passion. What can you give him? You're thin, small and washed out. He needs a real woman! Before long, he'll break it off with you and come crawling back to me. You mark my words!"

Molly was growing irritated with the dramatics. And, she suspected, if she had truly cared about Nick, she might have been upset to learn of a passionate affair. She'd never been involved in one herself and often envied other women when they gossiped about making mad, passionate love to their men.

"Well, if he does, more power to you. But I hardly think it's going to happen," Molly said, wondering how she could get rid of her unwanted guest. Was this part of being engaged to a hotel magnate? She wasn't impressed. Her first instinct had been the best—avoid the man at all costs. Why hadn't she listened?

"You will see!" With another dismissing glance around the art department, Carmen turned and walked away, but not before getting in the last word, "You have nothing. I can give him all he wants."

The silence was almost deafening as every eye watched her depart.

Two women near Molly laughed softly and applauded. "If the hunk who was in yesterday is the man you two are fighting over, good going, Mol," one said. "Who is she?"

"No one important," Molly sat back down, and stared at the layout. She was amazed at her calm reaction to Carmen's blatant attempts to cause a scene. She didn't do confrontations that well. Was this going to be something she had to expect while temporarily engaged to Nick Bailey?

Slipping away a few moments later, she called him.

She was put through immediately. His secretary was obviously another who thought the engagement was for real.

"Bailey."

"Hello, darling," she cooed. "I just couldn't wait until I saw you next to hear your voice. Is your day going as well as mine?"

"Molly?"

"Do you have other fiancées lurking around? Someone else Carmen can go harass?"

"Carmen? What's going on?"

"She wanted to make sure I knew what a passionate affair the two of you had. And how you'll be resuming it in the not too distant future once you dump me. Let's get one thing clear on this situation—when we end this farce, I get to dump you. I'm tired of being the dumpee."

"She came to your office?"

"Yes, but don't worry. I doubt she'll be back. She was not impressed."

"I didn't expect her to do anything like that. I hope you played your part."

"Hey, I live to please. But I would appreciate her not coming around again."

"I have no influence over her. If she'd accept our engagement is real, she'll turn her sights elsewhere."

"My guess is she'll hold out—hoping once the engagement ends she can step back in," Molly said thoughtfully.

"Carmen's not that patient."

"How patient does she need to be? We're not going to be engaged that long. Your mother will be well in no time."

"Don't keep talking about ending the engagement, someone will overhear you."

"No one can overhear. I wouldn't be holding this conversation with an audience!"

"Not now, but if you stay in that mind set, you'll let it slip when someone is around," he warned.

"Oh, gee, that would be too bad."

"I can make sure it is." That hint of steel came across loud and clear.

"Another threat. Honestly, Nick, is that how you go through life? I'm your fiancée, show some adoration." She almost laughed, imagining his face on the other end.

"You're right. I'll pick you up for dinner tonight. We'll practice being adoring and captivated. Your performance last night left something to be desired."

"What? I did great. Your mom is convinced I adore you." Molly was startled at the extent his comment bothered her. What kind of performance had he expected?

"You tighten up every time I touch you. People truly in love would be more comfortable around each other."

"You'd probably know more about that than I do, having had such a passionate affair with Carmen."

"Forget Carmen. You need practice."

"And you don't?"

"So we'll both practice. Seven o'clock okay?"

Molly agreed to the time and hung up. Her heart skipped a beat in anticipation. Just what kind of practice did Nick have in mind? Something that would make them more comfortable around each other—like more kisses? Sheesh, his kisses had done everything but make her *comfortable!*

Nick couldn't believe he was having dinner with Molly again. Or that he'd insisted. He'd seen her Wednesday night at the reception, last night at his mother's place, and had plans to see her tomorrow night at the charity ball. Tonight was overkill.

But Molly McGuire frankly intrigued him. She was unlike anyone he'd met in years. Feisty and focused, she had a balance that was missing from women like Carmen. The last thing he thought of when thinking of Molly was mercenary.

In fact, when thinking of Molly, it was hard to remember anything except her bright eyes, her irreverent attitude, her smart mouth.

A mouth he couldn't wait to kiss again.

Rising, he paced to the window, looking out across the expanse of Union Square to the glimpse of the bay. He couldn't see her apartment in China Basin, but he knew the general area. Not that she was home.

He shifted to look toward the financial district and the high-rises that held Zentech's offices. Tall buildings filled his view. Which one was Molly's? Thoughtfully he studied the buildings. Was she playing a deep game? Or was she as open as she seemed.

He didn't see how she could have set up their first encounter, yet stranger things had happened. Maybe she'd heard rumors and set out to see what would happen.

He shook his head. There was no way she could have known about Carmen.

Yet—he couldn't help think how their pictures had been in the paper. How much a splash the news had made of his supposed engagement. Molly McGuire would bear watching.

But as long as she didn't cause a problem, he'd continue the charade. His mother's recovery was of primary importance. If having her believe he was engaged to Molly speeded that recovery, he'd keep the engagement going indefinitely.

And, if last night was any indication, his mother would surprise them all with a miraculous convalescence and be back to her normal self in a short while. Time enough then to end his involvement with Molly.

In the meantime, they would be forced together by the nature of their deception. Donny was looking into her background. Nick wasn't one to take things on surface value. He liked full facts and figures. Still, there was no sense wasting an opportunity. He hadn't gotten where he was in business by ignoring opportunities when they unexpectedly appeared, but ruthlessly exploited them when they suited his ends.

Promptly at seven, Molly heard the knock on her door. She opened it, not surprised to find Nick on the other side. What did surprise her, however, was the flutter in her stomach when she saw him.

He seemed taller than she'd remembered. More formidable in the dark charcoal business suit and gray shirt. The subdued tie completed the understated but powerful look.

No smile lit his face. No sign of welcome.

"Ready?" he asked.

Molly nodded, wondering if she were a total idiot to spend the evening with him. If he was going to frown throughout dinner, she'd rather have take-out and eat alone!

"Is this okay?" she asked, motioning to the bright peacock blue dress. She had no idea where he planned to take her. Compared to his somber attire, she felt like a neon sign. But she liked bright colors.

His gaze drifted from her face down the length of her body. Molly felt the flutter kick into high gear.

"A simple yes or no would suffice," she snapped, afraid he'd see how his look affected her. The last thing she wanted to portray was her reluctant interest in the man. He was out of her realm, she knew that. Tonight should prove interesting.

"Yes."

She glared at him, miffed he hadn't said something more, like the color brought out the blue in her eyes, or he liked the way it brightened things up.

Not that this was a real date, she needed to remember that.

On the other hand, he had been the one to say they needed practice. Maybe he should start with compliments!

"You didn't say where we were going. Am I overdressed?" she asked as she stepped aside to allow him to enter. That would give him an opening.

"Depends on what your plans are." He reached out to cup her chin, tilting her face slightly and brushing a light kiss on her lips. "If you're going to bed, you're definitely overdressed."

"Dinner?" she said, annoyed to find her heart racing and her breathing labored from a slight kiss—and the image his words evoked. She had no business thinking of dark bedrooms, satin sheets. She'd never slept on satin sheets in her life! Darn, he was right, they needed practice to become comfortable together. "But kissing isn't the way to start."

"Start dinner?"

She frowned, realizing she'd said that last thought aloud. "No, start being comfortable," she stepped back, putting several feet between them. "I thought you said we needed practice to become comfortable around each other."

He nodded, watching her from narrowed eyes. "Touching, kissing, affectionate gestures in public. Practice."

"Right, but we're not in public now."

He shrugged, glancing around the open loft apartment. The ceiling rose twenty feet from the living area. The loft bedroom was built over the kitchen area where the ceiling was only ten feet high. The spaciousness was unexpected.

As were the colorful paintings on the wall, the eclectic mix of comfortable furniture. The floors were wooden, with rugs scattered here and there. It suited her, he thought, eyeing the circular stairs to the loft. What was her bedroom like?

The comment he'd made earlier had been designed to throw her. She fired up when teased. He was starting to look for the signs.

The dress she'd donned was perfect for an elegant dinner à deux. He noticed the way it fit snugly at the breasts, clung the length of her slender body. She wasn't as endowed as Carmen, but there was something femininely sexy about Molly that was missing from Carmen's flamboyant style. And at the moment, Nick found he preferred quiet elegance to flash.

Molly picked up a warm coat, the summer fog cooled the temperatures quickly after dark. Nick reached for it, his good manners showing.

He piqued her curiosity.

Despite being coerced into their engagement-of-convenience—and mostly Nick's convenience—she was fascinated by the man. Once they got to know each other a bit better, maybe some of that fascination would fade. But until then, she'd enjoy the mystery.

The biggest mystery being why he needed her to pretend to be a fiancée when he could probably have any woman in San Francisco jump at the chance.

CHAPTER FIVE

NICK was silent as they rode through the streets. Molly vowed she would not be the one to initiate conversation, and gazed around as if she'd never seen the city before. People were on their way home from work. A few stopped into the stores that were still open. As Nick drew closer to Little Italy, the stores and high-rises gave way to restaurants and nightclubs which would soon be bursting with customers. Friday nights were a time to cut loose.

He parked on Washington Square and looked at her.

"Italian suit you?"

"Fine."

She almost laughed at the wary look that came into his eye. She could be as succinct as he.

"What's the joke?" he asked.

"None. Just wondered if this was all part of your plan?"

"Plan?"

"You know, the practice makes perfect plan. 'Cause if it is, I have to tell you, you have a long way to go?"

"Indeed?"

"If this were a real date, don't you think you'd act differently?"

"This is a date. One where we can hammer out some rules for our engagement."

''Oh, gee, there you go again, sweeping a gal off her feet with romance.''

He leaned toward her, his eyes gleaming. ''Are you looking for romance?''

Molly was captivated by his gaze, her eyes locked with his. Once again she experienced that breathlessness, that flutter in her midsection. His dark eyes gleamed in sensuous awareness. What would it be like to have him romance her?

''No.'' Was she denying herself? Or him? She moved back, closer to the door, trying to break the spell that enveloped her. ''No, I'm not looking for romance. But you said we needed to practice. I would have expected more—finesse, I guess.''

''Finesse?'' He seemed startled. Then he laughed.

Molly blinked, caught by the change in his expression. Her heart skipped a beat. Heat flooded through her as she watched, mesmerized by the awareness that caught her by surprise. She could be attracted to this man. More than attracted.

She had better watch herself around Nick Bailey.

''My turn to ask what's funny.''

''I see I need to polish up my act,'' he said, reaching for the door handle. In a moment he was opening her door, ushering her from the car.

''Something tells me you wouldn't need much practice.''

''And what is that something?'' he asked, motioning to a small Italian restaurant across the street.

''I'm sure you have loads of experience.''

''You are giving me more credit than I deserve.''

''I don't know. I met Carmen, remember?

Definitely high maintenance. And I suspect she's not your first."

"I'm thirty-six years old, would you expect a man my age not to have dated?

"Dated? Ah, so that's what you call it. Carmen might be upset at so bland a description."

His jaw tightened. "I really don't want to spend our evening discussing Carmen. I'd rather spend it discussing you."

"Me?" Molly said in surprise.

They reached the double doors to the restaurant. Entering, they were immediately in the thick of a small crowd.

"Damn, I forgot it was Friday night," Nick murmured. Moving to the maître d's station, he glanced at the list the man was reviewing.

"It'll be a wait," he warned.

Molly shrugged. "I don't mind."

When he gave his name to the maître d', however, the man beamed at him. "Mr. Bailey, this is indeed a pleasure. I'm pleased to see you and your fiancée. Come this way, I have the perfect table for you."

Dumbfounded, Molly followed, ignoring the mumbles of disgruntled people behind her.

In seconds they were seated in a small table for two, in a secluded alcove. It was quiet, elegant and obviously one of the best tables in the house.

Presented with a menu, Molly hid behind it until the man left.

She peeped over it at Nick.

"Must be nice to have a friend in the right place."

"Never saw the man before that I remember. But I have eaten here a time or two."

Molly dropped her gaze to the menu. Had the man seen the paper and remembered? Even if he had, why seat them immediately?

"Does this happen often?" she asked, laying the menu aside. She knew she'd have the veal, she always did when eating Italian—it was her favorite.

"What?"

"Going to the head of the pack."

Nick shrugged and placed his menu on top of hers. "Sometimes, if they know who I am and think it'll get them something."

"A big tip?"

"A recommendation from our hotel when out of town visitors ask for a good place to eat."

"Ummm, that could be fun. Maybe we should eat out often while this engagement lasts. I bet I'll see some places I've never seen before."

Nick stiffened almost imperceptibly, but Molly noticed.

"What?"

"What do you mean?"

Her eyes narrowed as she studied him across the table. "You didn't like that comment. What set your back up?"

"Let's just say I have certain reservations."

"About?"

"About the whole setup."

She blinked and leaned back in her chair. "What setup? Our fake engagement?"

"Two days ago I didn't know you. Now the entire city of San Francisco believes we are engaged. I'm still waiting to find out what you expect from this?"

She rolled her eyes and frowned at Nick. "You

drive me crazy! I needed someone for the Zentech reception—one night only! You're the one perpetuating this engagement. Why do you persist in thinking I'm trying to get something from you? Are you always this suspicious and cynical?"

"Always, it keeps trouble at bay."

Molly ignored him, rummaging around in her small purse. She withdrew an index card, and a pen, and began scribbling on it.

"What are you doing?" Nick asked.

"I don't know if this is legal, but it should be. I'm disavowing any claim on anything of yours." She signed it with a flourish and tossed it across the table.

"If that doesn't suit you," she said tightly, "then consider our engagement off, and figure out how to tell your mother!"

He looked at the note.

The waiter arrived. Nick slipped the card into his jacket pocket while the man placed the water glasses on the table.

"Ready to order?" the waiter asked.

Once their selections had been given, Nick looked at Molly. Color remained high in her cheeks. Her eyes held an angry sparkle. He shouldn't bait her, but he continued to be intrigued by her reactions. The limited time they would spend together for this engagement should prove interesting.

"Nick Bailey, I thought it was you." A tall man dressed in business attire came to the table. "Congratulations, I read about your engagement in the paper. This is your fiancée?"

Nick rose and shook hands with the man and nodded. ''Molly, I'd like you to meet Jason Holton. Jason, Molly.''

Jason smiled at her. ''Nice to meet the woman who finally captured our friend. None of us thought we'd ever see the day. When's the wedding?'' He looked at Nick, ''I expect it'll be the biggest one San Francisco has ever seen, think of all who will crash the event just to see the impossible happen.''

''Nick has proved elusive in the matrimonial stakes, has he?'' Molly asked, amused by the embarrassment Jason heaped on his friend.

''He plays the field like—'' Jason suddenly realized to whom he was talking. ''Uh, you know how it is until a man finds the right woman.''

''Maybe you should return to Celeste and let Molly bask in her ignorance of my past,'' Nick suggested dryly.

''We're just starting dinner, maybe we can get together for a drink when we are all finished,'' Jason suggested.

''We have plans,'' Nick said firmly.

Jason glanced to Molly, back to Nick. ''Sure, sure, I understand. Another time.'' He slapped Nick on the back and nodded to Molly. ''You can meet Celeste next time. Congratulations, you two.''

Molly waited until he was out of earshot, then leaned forward to speak quietly.

''Just how is it until a man finds the right woman?''

Nick raised one eyebrow. ''I believe that's the kind of thing he'd never bring up once he has found the right woman.''

''And here you were trying to tell me you didn't have that much experience.''

"Jason exaggerates. He and Celeste married right out of college, and he still feels he's missing something by not playing the field."

"And is he?"

Nick shook his head. "I think they have a happy marriage, there's never been a hint of rumor about them. Still, there is the grass is greener feeling. I'm one of his last friends to still be single."

"And why is that?" Suddenly Molly realized she truly wanted to know about the man. Not for answering questions that might come up, but to satisfy her own curiosity. She knew what color he liked, what his favorite food was, but there was so much she didn't have a clue about.

Not that she needed to get too involved. This temporary engagement was likely to end as suddenly as it started. But until then, she'd satisfy that curiosity and find out as much about Nick Bailey as she could.

He shrugged. "At the age most men start looking for a mate, I was struggling to take control of Magellan Hotels. My father died suddenly of a heart attack. I had barely started work for the chain. I thought I had decades to learn the ropes, ease my way up the chain of command until I took over for my father. Instead, at age twenty-five, I was the majority stockholder and successor to my father."

"You're trying to tell me you haven't dated for the past ten years?"

"Of course not. But the kind of dates I had weren't the kind leading to marriage. A date for a business event, or charity affair."

"Or just for fun?" she asked.

He nodded. "Or for fun."

"But not the kind of women you take home to mother."

"The minute a man takes a woman home to meet his mother, he never hears the end of it."

Molly smiled, trying to envision Nick as a browbeaten man, plagued by his mother's prodding if he ever brought a woman home. Somehow the picture didn't gel. Nick had never been browbeaten in his life!

"Something tells me you could have stood up to your mother."

"Not lately." He leaned forward. "I still don't know what you want out of all this, but I'll do almost anything to get my mother well again."

Molly looked at him, wondering who had taken so much, he couldn't understand that some people would help out just as a kindness. He was convinced she was a mercenary. Would he ever see her differently?

"Guess you'll have to wait and see, won't you?" she asked, knowing it would drive him crazy—waiting, wondering. The thought boosted her morale like nothing else could have.

"A word of warning. I'm not a pushover. Be careful or you could be the one ending up hurt."

Molly almost wished she had just gone to the reception alone and faced Brittany and Justin without the elaborate scheme that seemed to have backfired. Almost, but her interest in Nick was growing as she learned tidbits about him. For now, he needed her.

After a delicious meal, and excellent service, they left. Waving to Jason and Celeste, on their way out, Molly was glad they were not going to have drinks with friends of Nick's. It was one thing to pretend to his mother while she was bedridden, something else again to keep up the facade with friends who knew the man well, and would know instantly she wasn't his type. Friends were more likely to be analytical than his mother.

As Molly slipped into the front seat of the car a few moments later, she was struck by the lack of practice. Hadn't that been his reason for taking her to dinner? Instead, they had chatted almost amicably over dinner, their talk innocuous at best. He had not held her hand. Had not kissed her. Had not called her sweetheart or darling or anything romantic even when the waiter served as audience.

When Nick slid in behind the wheel, she half turned to look at him.

"So what about this practice you talked about?"

"Anything special in mind?" he asked lazily. He looked at her. It was dark, the only illumination from the streetlights and neon signs on the nightclubs and restaurants along the perimeter of the Square.

If anything, the shadows and dim illumination made him seem even more the pirate. Molly shivered in delightful anticipation. Could she hold her own?

"You brought it up."

"What did you have in mind?"

"Primarily getting to know each other a bit better—so you aren't so jumpy when around me," he said lazily.

"I am not jumpy!"

He leaned closer, sliding his hand behind her neck. Molly's heart sped up, beating in double time. Mesmerized by the dark eyes that held hers, she tried for a deep breath. Her skin tingled where his warm palm touched. All coherent thought fled, her senses went on full alert.

"So if I kiss you, you'll be fine with it?" he asked.

Fine was hardly the word to use, she thought. Ecstatic, wild, excited, thrilled might come close. Not that she'd share that with the arrogant man. Time he was taken down a peg or two.

"I'll be fine with it," she said, leaning closer herself. "The question is will you?"

She closed the scant inches between them and placed her lips against his. Almost smiling at the start of surprise she detected, she gave her best shot.

In a flash, Nick took control of the kiss, drawing her close, opening his mouth and feeding the growing passion with his expertise. Deepening the kiss, he encircled Molly with his arms. She clutched his shoulders, holding on for dear life lest she spin away.

A kaleidoscope of colors exploded behind her closed eyelids, her senses floated, expanded. She was aware of his scent, his touch, his heat. His tongue danced with hers, drawing a deeper response. Her heart beat heavy, she could feel his pounding. The temperature rose dramatically until Molly wished she could open a window and let in the night fog to cool down.

But not if it meant moving away from the kiss.

If only it would continue forever. What magic had he wrought that she forgot good sense and longed for what couldn't be?

Endless moments later, Molly eased back and looked up at Nick. She cleared her throat, wishing she felt sophisticated and urbane and had a clever repartee. But mostly she wanted to throw herself against him again and kiss him until morning.

"Maybe this isn't such a great idea," she said. "I know you want practice and all, but I think that's all I need for tonight."

Nick rubbed her damp lips with one thumb, leaned back, and glanced around.

"Dammit, I can't believe I forgot where we are. Parked right on Washington Square in the middle of a Friday evening. Half of San Francisco could have driven by."

"It's dark. No one could see in the tinted windows," she said practically, leaning back, feeling suddenly cold. He could have said something to lighten the mood. Instead, he was back to frowning again.

He started the car and smoothly moved into the street, heading back to China Basin and her apartment. Molly didn't initiate any conversation, and Nick was decidedly quiet.

She gazed at the lights, trying not to dwell on the blood still rushing through her, or the tingling awareness that seemed to fill every cell. They had shared a kiss. Big deal.

But it was, she thought, still feeling the excitement. She had never felt quite like this before. Was it from kissing a man she scarcely knew? Forbidden fruit, so to speak? Or was there something special about Nick Bailey?

She didn't feel he was an easy man to know. He ruthlessly commandeered her cooperation in the charade, yet for loving reasons that seemed at such odds with his reputation. After *he* suggested the scheme, he doubted her enough to have her investigated. Yet his manners tonight had been attentive and interested.

Molly's street was empty of traffic when Nick turned on it. Parking, however, was a different matter. There was not a vacant space for two blocks. When they reached Molly's apartment building, Nick double parked and looked at her.

"I won't come up, if that's all right."

Molly stifled a short laugh. The last thing she wanted was anything more of Nick tonight. Tomorrow evening was time enough to deal with her raging hormones and gain a modicum of control. She wouldn't be responsible for the consequences if he kissed her again tonight.

"That's fine. I'll see you tomorrow, then."

"The cocktail hour starts at seven, I'll swing by about fifteen minutes before that. It won't take long to get to the hotel where they're holding it," he said, watching her with hooded eyes. "It's formal."

She nodded and opened her door. "I expected as much. Thanks for dinner. It was—interesting." She slid out before he could say anything and hurried to the front door.

"Molly?"

She turned. He'd gotten out of the car and looked at her over the top. "That kiss earlier—it wasn't just about practice."

She stood in amazement as he slid back behind the wheel, gave a casual wave, and drove off.

Early Saturday morning, Nick took a deep breath of cool air. The scent of eucalyptus and the sea mingled, filling his lungs with energy. He leaned over, stretching. Pushing against his car, he warmed muscles he'd need for his run.

Running in Golden Gate Park was something he didn't do as often as he'd like anymore. There was a five kilometer course he enjoyed that took him through some of the quietest parts of the park, and even had a stretch along the beach.

A dark Jeep pulled in behind him and Donny climbed out.

"Couldn't you find another time and place," he grumbled, walking over to Nick, sipping coffee from a take-out place.

"Nope." Nick looked him over, faded shorts, scuffed running shoes, and baggy T-shirt. Donny and he dressed alike.

"Ready to go?"

"No, I have to finish my coffee." Donny leaned against the car and closed his eyes. "Unlike you, I was up until three this morning." He opened one eye and looked at Nick. "I assume unlike you. What time did you take Molly home?"

"Long before three." Nick reached out and snagged the cup, flipping off the top and taking a long drink.

"Hey, that's mine."

"Sooner finished, sooner we can start," Nick said, handing it back. "Learn anything?"

"About Molly or the bar?"

"Either, both." Nick tried to keep his tone neutral, but he was curious about anything Donny might have found out about Molly. Curious and wary.

"Nada. She's clean."

"I don't need cop talk. I didn't think she was involved in some crime. Do you think she's got a plan in mind by going along with this scheme?''

''The only thing I can come up with is she's never been involved long term with anyone. I don't think she's trying to rip you off. There's no pattern to show that. And women in their late twenties don't just turn to conning people. She'd have to have experience before now if that was her goal.''

Nick nodded, turning and looking down the path. He had known Molly wasn't a con, but it was good to have it verified.

''Let's go,'' he said, starting to run.

Donny caught up in a second and the two men began to pace themselves, falling into the familiar routine with ease.

''And the bar?'' Nick asked.

''Something definitely going down there, cuz, and I think it's Harry Coker.''

''Harry? He's been there for two years. We only noticed the shortages about eight months ago,'' Nick said.

''So you said. However, things change. I'm running a background check. Maybe something came up eight months ago to turn him.''

''Do you know for sure it's Harry?''

''I'm getting proof.'' They ran in silence for a short while. ''You going to prosecute when I get it?''

''Damn straight I am.''

''Figured you would. What if it's a kid who needs an operation or something?''

''Find out what's going on and leave the consequences to me,'' Nick ordered.

''Aye, Boss. Besides I'm not nearly as interested

But it was always her day—a treat to herself for putting up with clients and account executives and bosses who sometimes expected miracles, and who all thought of art as a commodity rather than a creative process.

She liked working for Zentech, but she loved painting. Her dream was to one day be able to support herself solely by her art. But that day hadn't arrived.

She had several pictures currently hanging in two galleries in town, one near the wharf, one near Union Square. Both small establishments, both still growing in reputation. The paintings she'd already sold helped augment her salary, enabling her to buy her flat when the building had changed from rentals to purchases. Her hobby, as her parents called it, enabled her to vacation in exotic locales—which she of course immediately set about to capture in oil.

Today she wanted to put the finishing touches on a painting she'd been doing in Golden Gate Park for several weekends—of a section of the Japanese Tea Garden. The weeping willow tree's airy branches drifted toward the water, a small stone bridge arched over the stream. Done primarily in shades of green and brown, she was pleased with the way it was coming.

She wore comfortable jeans, a soft cotton top covered by her paint-splattered smock. It was warm enough she didn't need shoes. Her ablutions this morning had consisted of a quick shower and brushing her teeth. Her hair had dried wavy after a quick combing and she pulled it into a ponytail to keep it out of the way.

She studied the canvas, head tilted slightly to the

right, as she decided just where a bit more work was needed. A couple of hours and she'd be done. She reached for the oils.

Normally as soon as she touched brush to paint she was lost in a world of color and texture and shape. But today the comfort zone didn't appear. She dabbed a leaf, and thought about Nick and his kiss. She studied the water, but saw instead the two of them at dinner last night. Despite her best efforts, she had not learned as much about him as she wanted. He was either a champion at dissembling, or more reserved than she'd suspected.

Once again, she dragged her attention to the canvas. She did not want to keep thinking about Nick. Today was her only day to devote fully to painting. She had chores to do around the place tomorrow and then the workweek started.

What was Nick doing today? Did he spend it in the office? At a golf course? Sailing? Shouldn't she know the very basics of a supposed-fiancé's hobbies? Stopping in the midst of painting when she didn't have to was almost unheard of, but she put down the palette and brush and went to rummage through her purse.

She pulled out the paper Donny had prepared. She'd glanced through it when going to Nick's mother's house the other day, but not absorbed everything. She reread it quickly. Just as she thought—Donny hadn't listed leisure activities.

Fat lot of good that report was, she fumed, returning to the easel. She resumed touching up the painting, her mind half focused on the work, half on wondering about Nick Bailey.

CHAPTER SIX

SOMETIME later the phone startled her. She rarely got calls on Saturday—most of her friends knew her only-day-to-really-paint. If it were a telemarketer, she'd really be annoyed, she thought as she put down the brush and went to answer.

"Hello?"

"Molly, Ellen Bailey. I hope I'm not calling at a bad time." The voice sounded stronger through the phone than it had the other evening.

"Now is fine. How are you?"

"Much better, thank you. I know it's short notice, but I am feeling strong enough to have company for lunch. Would you join me? It will give us a chance to get to know each other—without worrying about Nick."

"Worrying about Nick?"

Ellen laughed softly. "Well, we can't really talk about everything we want if he's sitting here with us, now can we?"

Molly became intrigued. "And what would we be wanting to talk about without him?"

"How he was as a little boy, for one. I have some albums if you are interested in seeing some old family photographs."

Molly glanced at the painting. It was finished, she was merely holding on to it because she always hated to finish a project. Until she was consumed by a new project, she felt let down, at loose ends.

"If you have other plans, I'd understand," Ellen said with dignity.

Molly didn't have other plans, or any real reason to refuse, except she didn't wish to become more involved. But the loneliness in the woman's tone touched her. How much would it take to spend a couple of hours with Ellen Bailey?

"No, I have no other plans. What time shall I come?"

"Twelve-thirty would be fine." She gave Molly directions, then hung up.

Molly hesitated a moment, then tried to call Nick at the hotel. She was mildly surprised to discover he didn't work on Saturdays. And there was no one there to tell her where he might be.

"The least he could have done was given me his cell phone number, or even his home number," she grumbled, as she tried in vain to find a listing in the phone book. Another thing to discuss. This being engaged was growing more complex.

She worried about how Nick would react when he discovered Molly and his mother had shared a meal without him.

"Probably suspect me of trying to con her out of his inheritance," she thought, picturing his annoyance.

"Oh well, that'll teach him to keep his fiancée in the dark!"

Molly was shown into Ellen's bedroom upon arrival. The older woman was wearing a lacy champagne colored peignoir and propped up on a dozen pillows. She beamed a warm welcoming smile when Molly entered. Even in such a short time, Molly could see improvement.

"I'm so glad you came, Molly. Forgive me for not getting up. I tried it, and it was so much of a strain, I decided it would be better to rest and devote my energy to our visit, rather than sitting in a chair, or taking the stairs."

"This is fine. If my being here tires you out, let me know and I'll leave." Molly glanced at Mrs. Braum, the nurse. The woman smiled her greeting and retired to sit near the windows.

"Having you here is like a tonic. Would you like something to drink?"

"I'll wait for lunch. How are you feeling?" Molly sat in the straight chair near the bed. Ellen still looked almost as frail as she had the other night. Molly suspected she'd lost a lot of weight while sick, and that part of her recovery delay was due to lack of energy. She needed to rebuild her reserves.

"Much better, thank you. Oh dear, I noticed the other night you weren't wearing an engagement ring. I was hoping you'd just left it home or something. Didn't I see one in the newspaper photographs?"

"Uh," Molly tried to think. She hoped her expression didn't give her away. She was not good at subterfuge. "Actually I have a lovely ring, but I don't wear it when painting, I don't want to get oils on it. I was painting when you called. I forgot to put it back on when I cleaned up."

She was going to have to remember to wear her grandmother's ring!

"I can't wait to see it. Tell me again how you and Nick met and when he proposed. Was it a total surprise? Was he romantic?" Ellen asked wistfully.

"Donny introduced us," Molly said, hoping she wasn't going to be questioned to death. What had he told his mother? How awful if they got their stories mixed up. "Not too long ago, actually. It's been a whirlwind romance." To say the least.

"I would love to hear about Nick as a boy," Molly said. The key to getting through lunch was to have Ellen talk about Nick, freeing Molly to just listen. No way to make a faux pas doing that!

"Mrs. Braum, would you bring me that first album," Ellen said.

The nurse rose and brought the album. "I'll run downstairs and see how Shu-Wen is doing with lunch. I believe it'll be ready shortly."

"We'll be here," Ellen said dryly. When the nurse left, Ellen smiled at Molly. "She's a dear, but I think it's time she moved on. As soon as I can, I'll be back on my feet and ready to help with the wedding. I'm looking forward to meeting your parents, too. Were they thrilled their daughter is getting married?"

"They, um, don't know about the engagement."

"Why not?"

"They're on a cruise right now. It's sort of hard to reach them." Of course Molly had their itinerary and contact information, but she would not be telling them about this engagement. With any luck, it would all be over before they returned home.

"I'm sure they'd love to hear from you," Ellen said slowly, studying Molly thoughtfully.

Molly nodded and smiled brightly, pointedly looking at the album. "Do you have baby pictures of Nick?"

When the door flung open a few moments later, Molly, Ellen and Mrs. Braum all looked up in surprise. The three women had been examining the photographs in the album. Molly had been absorbed by the glimpses of Nick as a child. He'd looked like a mischievous kid. When had he acquired that serious air?

Nick stood in the doorway, surveying them all with disbelief.

"Molly, what are you doing here?" he asked.

"Visiting your mother," she replied, her gaze taking him in. Gone was the immaculately attired business mogul. Gone the Armani suits and wing tip shoes. Instead, he looked even more like her disreputable pirate. Running shorts displayed his muscular legs, his hair was mussed as if he'd been in a wind tunnel, and the way his T-shirt stretched across an impressive chest almost had her salivating.

He'd obviously been doing something physical and on him it looked great.

Her eyes met his and saw the suspicion.

Here we go again, she thought, glancing at Mrs. Braum and his mother. Had they noticed?

"We're looking at the family album," she said to fill the silence.

"What are you doing here, Nicholas?" his mother asked.

"I got a call from Shu-Wen. She said I was to come right away. I thought something had happened."

Ellen made a tsking sound. "I asked her to call you

to let you know Molly was here. I invited her for lunch. I thought you might wish to drive her home later. But it wasn't an emergency."

"Molly's staying for lunch?"

"Yes."

From the glare Molly received from Nick, it didn't take a rocket scientist to figure out he did not want her to stay. She was trying her best to think as a fiancée would think. What did Nick expect her to do when his mother invited her?

"Then I'll change and join you both. Maybe I could see Molly for a minute."

Ellen relaxed and smiled broadly. "Of course."

Molly wished she could smile. She knew Ellen was imagining a passionate greeting between lovers. Instead, as she followed Nick into the hall, she feared retribution. He closed the bedroom door, isolating them in the hall.

"What game are you playing now?" he asked in a hard tone.

"Umm, that would be the one you started, I believe—fool your mother for as long as it suits you?"

"I mean here. Why did you come here this morning? Did you honestly think I wouldn't find out?"

She was getting a bit annoyed by his constant suspicions. "She invited me. I demurred. She insisted. Weren't you the one trying to get her better ASAP? I think she's lonely. And bored. I'm a diversion."

"Bored? She has tons of friends. She could call one of them."

"How about her doting son?"

"I don't ignore her. We're not talking about me. I

don't want you with my mother when I'm not around, is that clear?''

''Why not?''

He ran his hand through his hair in pure frustration. ''Just leave it at that. I'll go change and join you shortly.''

Daringly Molly danced her fingertips up one muscular arm. ''Don't change on my account,'' she said teasingly. She almost laughed at the startled look on Nick's face. It was priceless. Maybe she should start playing the role of fiancée and see if that was what he really wanted.

He caught her fingers in his hand, squeezing gently, holding on.

''Now what?'' he almost growled.

''The angle? Aren't you always looking for an angle? Why not try trusting sometime,'' Molly asked.

''I learned fast that trusting in life can get you kicked in the teeth.''

''Gee,'' she leaned closer, ''we wouldn't want that to happen, you have such nice teeth.''

''All the better to bite with,'' he replied, drawing her closer until he pulled her into his arms.

''And do you bite?'' she asked, daring him with her smile, her pulse racing in anticipation.

''Sometimes.'' He watched her every second it took for him to slowly lower his head until his lips touched hers.

He tasted warm and male and slightly salty. She wrapped her arms around his neck and held on as he deepened the kiss. He was strong, solid, muscular and hot. She caught the heat from him, almost bursting into flames.

Nick knew he should stop. He didn't want any more involvement with Molly McGuire than necessary. But she was so soft in his arms. Her mouth so sweet, the way she kissed inflamed him. He wanted to sweep her away, take her to his room and keep them occupied for a week.

The thought shocked him. Slowly he eased back, resting his forehead on hers, watching her eyes flutter and then open.

"Done?" she asked.

She had a sassy mouth. He wanted to kiss it again. "I'll join you two as soon as I change."

"Do you have to go home to change?" Her voice was low, husky. Nick didn't want to move an inch.

"No, I have some things here. I won't be long."

"Then I'll try to contain myself until you join us." Molly stepped back, brushed down the front of her shirt and reached to open the door.

"Careful what you say to my mother," he warned.

"We're just looking at baby pictures. You were a cute little boy, were you also as suspicious then of everything?"

"Life teaches some hard lessons."

"I can't imagine anyone teaching you anything." Molly replied with a saucy grin. "But you'll be happy to know I'm getting good at this pretending. It's the practice, you know." She opened the door and stepped in as if she belonged.

He wanted to follow her immediately, watch everything she did, make sure she wasn't trying to worm her way into his mother's graces enough to wreak havoc. Molly knew his mother was fragile, was she somehow planning to take advantage of that?

Nick showered and changed in record time. He didn't trust Molly. He'd been out in the real world long enough to know women wanted him for the money he had to spend, the good time he could show them. Loyalty and love had little to do with anything these days.

As he walked along the hall toward his mother's room, he tried to remember just when he had become so distrustful around women. When Gillian Prentice had jilted him his senior year in college? Or after the play Marissa Bellingham had made shortly following his takeover of Magellan Hotels? He still owed his friend Hamilton for arranging for him to hear her admit she only wanted to marry him for the potential earnings he had. That had been a blow. Since then, cynicism had served him well. Each woman whom he dated knew right up front he was not interested in marriage. Even Carmen, much as she would like to change the rules.

There was no reason to suspect Molly was any different. To the contrary, there was a wider gap between the two of them than the women he usually dated. She lived in a small apartment in China Basin. He lived on Nob Hill. She painted to supplement her income. He had the family fortune at his back.

Donny may think she was on the up and up, but Nick suspected she'd seen a ripe opportunity fall into her lap and was taking every advantage.

He'd put up with it to help his mother—but watch her like a hawk.

Opening the door, he was surprised to see his mother laughing. She had color in her cheeks. Her eyes sparkled when she looked at Nick with delight. The change was almost miraculous.

"There you are. Come in and listen to Molly tell about painting her apartment."

He pulled a chair over and sat close enough to Molly his knee touched hers. When she shifted slightly to end the contact, he leaned over and put his hand on the back of her chair.

Just like he's staking a claim for all to see, Molly thought wishing Nick wouldn't crowd her space. She had been doing her best to entertain Ellen, but now she felt tongue-tied as awareness of Nick threatened to swamp her.

"I thought you painted pictures," he murmured.

She gave him a look and shifted a bit to the left. "I do paint pictures, but I wanted to brighten up my flat from the first moment I moved in. The walls were some dreary green. I wanted them bright and cheery."

"Tell him about your makeshift scaffolding," Ellen urged.

Molly looked uncertainly at Nick. Not for him some makeshift arrangement, she suspected. Heck, he'd hire a battery of painters if he wanted any color changes.

"Well, you know my place has a loft, so the walls on three sides go up almost twenty feet."

He nodded. He had only been inside that one time, but he remembered the layout.

"I borrowed my neighbor, Shelly's, table and put hers and mine side by side, then put up a couple of chairs and had a board running between them. It worked great."

He stared at her. ''You could have fallen and broken your neck.''

''It was a pain to move it every time I needed to change places, but it worked perfectly. And saved a ton of money. I had a painter give me an estimate, and it was lots more than I wanted to pay.''

Nick could picture her on the makeshift scaffolding, and envision her setup collapsing, tumbling her to the floor with chairs and board crashing down on top of her.

''Don't do it again,'' he said sharply.

Molly looked at him. ''What?''

''It's too dangerous. Don't do it again.''

''I was very careful,'' she said.

''And it was before she met you, Nick,'' Ellen said. ''I'm sure the need won't arise again, will it? After all, Molly won't be living there much longer. We haven't discussed your wedding at all, but don't hold off because of me. I'm feeling stronger every moment. And to have a definite date will spur me on to recover even faster.''

Molly looked at Nick, her eyes wide. Now what? They dare not set a date, no telling what Ellen would do. But how did they stall without giving away their charade?

''We want to wait for Molly's parents to return. Once they do, we can all get together and discuss things. They don't even know we're engaged,'' Nick said easily.

Grateful for the reprieve, Molly smiled at him. ''Clever,'' she mouthed in approval. Turning back to Ellen, she nodded. ''I'm sure you understand I want to talk to them before Nick and I move forward. This has been a whirlwind romance, you know."

"But one that was meant to be. You two are perfect together."

Once lunch was finished, Nick urged his mother to rest telling her he'd take Molly home.

When they reached the lower level in the house, Molly stopped him. "You don't have to you know, I can call a cab."

"I want to talk to you."

"Oh-oh, another lecture?"

He frowned. "I do not give lectures."

She laughed and patted his arm, aware of the strength of his muscles, the heat emanating from him. Then she turned, almost sighing for what couldn't be. For a split second Molly again wished things were different between her and this dynamic man. Wished she herself was more trusting, could believe men and women from such diverse backgrounds could meet and find common ground. But she'd been burnt trying that. She was on her guard.

And this wasn't even an attempt to find common ground. They'd entered into a pact to aid the recovery of an ill woman.

As they sped toward the wharf, she leaned back in the luxurious car and gazed idly out the window. She had enjoyed her visit, learned a lot about Nick. And connected with Ellen Bailey in a curious way. The woman seemed to be a mix of haughty grandeur and loneliness.

"What did you and my mother talk about?" Nick asked.

"This and that. Mostly about you as a boy. She thought I'd want to know all about you. She doesn't seem to think she was a great mother—more concerned about her antiques than letting a little boy run wild in the house."

"She was a fine mother."

"And she wishes she had more children. A little girl, definitely."

He flicked a glance her way. "I never knew that. I thought one was all she wanted."

"She said she and your father both hoped for more, but it wasn't to be. She also misses your father a great deal. He died ten years ago, and she's still lonely for him. That's sweet in a sad way."

"She has friends. Charity work."

"Nick, they were married twenty-seven years. He was the love of her life. Of course she'd miss him. She'll probably always miss him."

"She could get married again."

"Only if she found someone she loved as much as your father. What do you think?"

"That all that love stuff is overrated and a bunch of hype. Men and women marry for various reasons. If their hormones are raging and they want to call it love, let them."

"Okay, you get the cynical man of the year award. But just because you don't believe in love, doesn't mean your mother doesn't. And she won't settle for less."

"And you, do you believe in love?"

Molly was silent for a long moment. "I want to," she said sadly. But truth to tell, she wondered if she'd ever find it. Infatuation was hard enough. Would she recognize life-time love if she ever stumbled upon it?

Maybe she just hadn't found the right mate for her. Her parents were happy. Ellen had been happy with her husband. Molly was twenty-eight years old and had thought a couple of times she'd found a man she could share her life with. With each disappointment disillusionment set in. Maybe she was expecting too much.

When Nick pulled to a space near her flat, she reached for the door handle. His hand on her left arm stopped her.

"I'll pick you up tonight around six forty-five."

"I'll be ready."

"I'll get the door," he said, opening his own and sliding from beneath the wheel.

He opened hers moments later.

"Until later," she said.

"Molly," he said as she started to walk toward her building.

"What?"

"There are going to be a lot of people there tonight watching to make sure this is for real. Including Carmen."

She grinned. "Don't worry, I'll wear the sexiest dress I have and be all over you like mustard on a hotdog."

He groaned slightly and shook his head. "Charming analogy."

She waved and walked away.

He stood watching her. She was sexy in jeans. What would she be like in a sexy dress? He was almost afraid to find out.

* * *

"So tell me again about this guy," Shelly said sometime later as she sprayed the hair style she'd just completed on Molly. She looked at her friend in the mirror.

"The last thing I remember, you were going to pretend to be engaged, flaunt your grandmother's ring in Justin's face and waltz through the reception. Next, I see your face in all the newspapers, complete with fiancé. Now you're going someplace where everyone who is anybody in San Francisco will see you, and you tell me it's all a scam?"

"Not a scam," Molly protested, touching one curl lightly. "This looks great! Thanks, Shelly." She crossed to her bed and took the dress, holding it up to her. "It's basic black, but it'll work, won't it?" she asked her neighbor.

"I remember when you bought it. You trying to put the make on this guy? He'll be drooling."

Molly laughed. "I don't think so. Stay around awhile and meet him. Mr. Business-is-Everything."

"That's why he's a gazillionaire."

Molly looked at Shelly. "He's rich, I know, but a gazillionaire?"

"Hey, he owns Magellan Hotels. That isn't chump-change. So maybe he's not Bill Gates, but he's still got to be rolling in dough. My mother always said it was as easy to fall in love with a rich man as a poor man."

"I'm not falling in love with anyone," Molly protested, slipping into the dress. It was a snug fit. She'd loved it the first time she'd seen it. With silver threads shimmering throughout, the dress drew attention like flames drew a moth. It was short, with thin straps baring her shoulders. The snug bodice faithfully outlined every inch of her body. She was glad she walked to work most days, to keep off the pounds. This dress would show even an extra ounce.

She slid her feet into the scarcely-there high-heeled sandals. Nick would still top her by a good six or eight inches, but she felt taller wearing them.

Shelly rummaged around her dresser top, and came up with crimson lipstick.

"This!" she announced. "That dress and your attitude cries out for red."

"My attitude?"

"The one you're adopting for your performance tonight. You've got to compete with Carmen, and who knows who else at this event."

"I'm not competing with anyone. This is a fake engagement. If Nick wants to move on to someone else, fine by me." But as she leaned closer to the mirror, applying the crimson red lipstick, she felt a twinge of jealousy. It shouldn't, but it did bother her to think he might be attracted to someone else.

Which was foolishness to the extreme. They had entered an engagement-of-convenience. It would not last. And she'd be an idiot to think for one second that Nick Bailey could be attracted to someone like her.

CHAPTER SEVEN

PROMPTLY at six forty-five, the doorbell rang.

"Businessmen obsess about time like they do everything else," Molly muttered as she crossed to open the door. She caught her breath when she saw Nick. He wore a tux. She'd thought he looked yummy enough to eat earlier that day in running attire, now she knew why women wanted men to wear tuxedos. Wow!

"Ready?" he asked, his gaze running down the length of her.

She wasn't sure, but she thought she saw a flare of heat in his eyes.

"Just about. Come in and meet my next door neighbor, Shelly." Molly quickly made introductions, amused by Nick's wariness and Shelly's open suspicion.

"It was your idea about the false engagement, wasn't it?" Nick asked.

Shelly nodded. "But you added a twist. In my scenario, there was no guy."

"It wouldn't have worked," he said.

"And this will? What happens when someone catches you two?"

"As long as it's after my mother recovers, no harm done," he shrugged.

"Don't mind me," Molly said, reaching for a light coat. "I do have some say in this."

in that as I am in what you're going to do about Molly."

"I'm not doing anything with her."

"Dates four nights this week sounds like something."

"How did you know about last night?"

"Hey, I'm the hot-shot investigator, remember."

They broke from the canopy of trees into the segment that ran parallel to the beach. The breeze was strong, keeping them cool even as they racked up another kilometer.

Nick thought about Donny's question as they pounded on the packed dirt path. What was he going to do about her?

That kiss last night had nothing to do with practice, and all to do with desire.

He hadn't felt like that around a woman since he'd been a randy teenager. Even when entangled in some affair, he was known to keep his cool.

But kissing Molly had blown that out the window. One of the hardest things he'd done recently was to leave her at her apartment and not go up with her.

"Want to share the joke?"

"What?" He looked at Donny.

"You're smiling. Some joke?"

"No." He was just wondering what she'd thought about his parting comment.

Saturdays were Molly's favorite day. She rose early, had a quick breakfast and then began to paint. Sometimes beside the floor to ceiling windows catching the north light. Sometimes on location, especially when the weather was good.

Nick looked at her, his expression impassive. ''Shall we go?''

''Have fun, and don't forget what my mother said!'' Shelly said, heading out of the flat before them. She waved and entered a door down the hall.

As Molly checked to make sure her own door was locked, Nick asked about Shelly's last comment.

Molly could imagine his expression if she told him. ''Nothing, just some motherly advice. Is there anything I should know before we get there, or am I to just wing it all night?''

''We'll be sitting with some friends. The Petersons and the Harrells. I've known both men for years. Tim Peterson's wife is his second, and they've only been married a few months. Betsy and Baxter Harrell have been married since college days.''

''Is that where you know them from? College?''

They reached the car and Nick opened the passenger's door for Molly. She shivered slightly in the cool night air. The fog had blanketed San Francisco bringing a damp chill. It also gave a luminescence to the city lights, diffusing them and mingling to provide an eerie overcast that glowed.

Nick joined her and soon had the car heading for a rival hotel where the charity ball was being held.

''Your friends?'' she reminded him. ''From college?''

''No.'' He flicked her a glance. ''From when we were boys.''

''They lived near you?''

''We saw each other at Mrs. Porters's Dance Academy, if you must know. My mother insisted I attend, as did the others.''

"Dance Academy?" Molly murmured.

"And if you breathe a word of that to anyone, heads will roll."

She laughed softly. "I'll keep that in mind. So both your long-time friends are married, but you're not."

"No."

"Ever been?"

"No."

"Ever going to be?"

He was silent for a moment. "I expect so, one day. Don't you?"

"Eventually, if I find the right man for me."

"And how will you know?"

"I'm hoping I'll recognize my soul mate when he shows up. Marriage is for so long, I sure don't want to make a mistake."

"Divorce is easy enough."

"Not for me. I'm getting married and planning to stay that way until we die. Like my folks. Like your parents. Your mother still loves your father, you know."

Nick didn't respond. Molly knew it wasn't because of traffic, it was light for a Saturday night in the city. Soon they were driving into the valet parking lane of the hotel.

She stepped out and waited for Nick, tucking her hand into his arm as they entered the hotel. From now on she had to remember she was the darling fiancée of a powerful man. She just hoped she could act convincingly enough to fool the world. Or at least Carmen Hernandez.

They found their table easily enough and Molly soon met Nick's long-time friends. She liked them both and was equally taken with their wives. Tim's second wife, Annessa, was years younger than the rest of them, even younger than Molly. She was friendly and pretty, and, Molly guessed, around twenty-three. Had Tim already gone through a midlife crisis and obtained a trophy bride? Molly glanced at Nick. Maybe waiting for the right mate made more sense. Molly didn't want to ever experience the heartbreak of divorce.

"It's not often Nick can surprise us, but he did with you," Tim said once introductions had been made. "Last I knew he was seeing—" He stopped suddenly and looked at Nick almost in panic.

"Carmen," Nick said easily. "Don't worry, Molly knows all about Carmen."

She leaned closer and flirtatiously smiled up at him. "All about her?" she said in a husky whisper meant to carry.

The others laughed. Nick's gaze locked with hers and for a moment, Molly felt as if there was only the two of them. His hand came up, as if he couldn't resist, and brushed against her cheek. "All the important stuff," he replied.

"Oh, oh she has him wrapped around her little finger already," Baxter said.

"Captivated," Nick said, his gaze never leaving hers.

Molly almost believed him. When he did fall for someone, that woman would know his devotion all her life. Lucky woman!

The music started. "Shall we?" Nick said rising.

The others protested they wanted to get to know

Molly better, but he merely smiled and took her hand, leading her to the dance floor.

"Next time tell them everything in advance. I feel like I'm constantly explaining the story of my life," Molly said as he swung her into his arms. They moved perfectly together.

"The academy paid off," she said as he expertly led them around the floor, moving in time to the rhythm, never bumping into others.

"This'll be a nine-day wonder, then everyone will forget. If I hadn't already agreed to come to this, we could have stayed away. But coming without you would have been impossible without giving rise to gossip in the local column that my mother would have picked up at once."

"She seemed better today."

"I agree. Which is why we continue a bit longer."

"I still think the letdown when we tell her will be a shock."

The song ended and they headed for their table. When they drew near, Molly saw Carmen sitting in the chair she'd had. She took a deep breath. Great, another confrontation from the Spanish Bombshell. Just what she wanted—not.

"Your friend is tenacious, I'll give her that," Molly said.

She felt Nick pause a moment, anger almost radiating. "It's going beyond tenacious."

"Hello, lover," Carmen said smiling smugly. She glanced around the table at the others, almost preening with every eye on her.

"I don't believe this is your table," Nick said.

"I don't believe you are engaged. We meant too

much to each other for you to fall madly in love with someone else in the few weeks we've been apart. If you are trying to make me jealous, I will confess you have succeeded. Now, get rid of her."

"Oh, boy," Tim said softly.

"Oh, Nicky, don't listen to her," Molly said, holding his arm, pressing against him with her breasts. "I love you. We were meant to be, don't let her get her clutches into you, darling. I couldn't bear it without you!"

He looked at her as if she'd lost her mind, then something clicked. Amusement danced in his gaze. Sweeping her into an embrace, he kissed her. His arms held her firmly. He leaned over slightly, tipping Molly back until she was totally relying on him for support. The music faded as blood began pounding through her veins. She forgot about their charade, could only feel the power of the man, the magnetism, the sexy attraction that she could never deny.

The kiss went on and on and on. Finally the rest of the world began to penetrate and Molly gave a soft moan of protest.

Nick stood, releasing her slowly, his eyes on her. "Does that convince you I'm totally captivated?" he asked.

For a second, Molly felt she was in two dimensions, one where Nick did care for her, and had shown the world. The other the narrow walk of deception, where they needed to fool everyone by whatever means necessary.

"I'm convinced," Betsy said.

"Me, too," Annessa said. "Tim, you never kiss me like that."

"Honey, I don't think anyone in the world was kissed like that before."

Carmen glared at them, pushing back and rising. She did not speak as she stormed away.

A lone clapping sounded and Molly looked at Baxter. "Good job, some people have to be hit on the head to get the message. But, Nick, you set a hard standard for the rest of us!"

Molly sat down in her chair and tried to join in the conversation that bantered about. But her mind was focused on the kiss. How long before her pulse returned to normal, she wondered. Unable to resist, she peeped at Nick from beneath her lashes. He was studying her. Maybe the others believed theirs was a love match. She smiled, hoping she looked like the adoring fiancée he wanted her to portray.

What she wanted was the safety of her own flat. Away from curious glances and conversational land mines. And away from the lure of Nick Bailey. She was getting the lines blurred between reality and fantasy. She knew she'd been the one to ask him to act captivated, but did he have to do such a good job? He couldn't distance himself a tad now that they'd convinced everyone they were in love. If she didn't keep a tight rein on herself, she was in danger of losing her head—and her heart.

"What is it you do for a living, Molly?" Annessa asked.

"I work as a graphic designer for Zentech," Molly replied, glad to focus on something beside Nick.

"Zentech, isn't that one of the leading high-tech firms in the Bay Area?" Baxter asked.

Molly nodded.

"So how did you and Nick meet?"

"Donny introduced us," Nick said easily, his hand on the back of Molly's chair, his fingertip gently tracing patterns on her shoulder.

Molly could hardly concentrate on the conversation. She was exquisitely aware of Nick touching her, and the shimmering sensations that danced on every nerve ending as a result. Did he have any idea what he was doing?

"So when's the big day?" Tim asked.

"We haven't decided yet," Molly said quickly. "My parents are on a cruise and we want to wait until they return before making any plans."

"How is your mother," Baxter asked Nick.

"Recovering, thanks."

"And is she happy her only son is getting married?" Betsy asked, smiling broadly. "I bet she can't wait to become a grandmother. At least that's what we hear from our parents all the time!"

Molly glanced at Nick and almost laughed at his stunned expression. Most people did expect to have children once they were married. He looked as if the idea had never crossed his mind.

"She hasn't said," he replied.

Waiters began weaving their way through the tables, beginning to serve the meal. Before long, the music changed, became softer, more conducive to conversation. At the end of the meal, brief speeches were made, and the total amount garnered for the Foundation was announced. Once the applause died down, the dance music began again and Nick took Molly's hand and led her to the dance floor.

"It's going well, don't you think?" she asked as

they began to move to the sensuous music. ''They all think I adore you,'' she said smugly. ''I'm a great actress. Maybe I missed my calling.''

He looked down at her and tightened his arms slightly. ''Don't get too complacent, I've known these people a long time.''

''And your point is?''

''I'm not sure they are convinced.''

She glanced at the table, but it was empty, the others dancing, as well. ''How can you say that? They think it was a whirlwind romance!''

''Maybe they bought into it tonight, but your not knowing about my apartment when they mentioned the view had Tim, at least, looking thoughtful.''

''So, if they learn the truth, they won't tell your mother, will they?''

''It's not that anyone would go up and ring the doorbell to tell her I'm not engaged, but word has a way of spreading. Look at the situation we're in.''

''Well I had no idea newspaper photographers would be at the reception, or have any interest in my phony engagement. Your cousin should have told me who you were instead of setting up the whole thing.''

''Maybe he thought you already knew.''

''Back to that again? Honestly Nick, I don't know how you make it through the day with all the suspicions you harbor.'' The joy of the dancing vanished. Molly tugged on his hand. ''I want to go home. We came, were seen, and insulted by your ex-lover. Your friends have been given a display of our deep and abiding love. So what's keeping us here?''

He pulled her closer. ''What's the rush? Don't you like dancing?''

"With someone I like."

He spun them around. "And I'm not in that category?"

She shrugged. Suddenly she smiled right into his eyes and murmured for his ears alone, "Carmen on my left."

A moment later, Molly spoke louder. "We could go back to my place, darling."

Nick knew it was for show, Carmen must be closer. But he was startled with the realization he wanted to go back to Molly's. That he was tired of the night, of dealing with image and power and manipulations. Molly's flat was quiet and unpretentious.

"Then let's say our goodbyes."

In only minutes, they were in Nick's car, heading toward China Basin. Molly relaxed against the seatback, still humming the last song. "All in all, I had a good time."

"You sound surprised, didn't you expect to?" Nick asked.

"No. This really isn't my kind of thing. I was worried I'd do something terrible and all your friends would pity you for getting engaged to me."

"Really?" That intrigued him. He couldn't imagine any other women he knew thinking that, or admitting it aloud. They'd have all been so excited to be seen with him, the last thing they would have cared about was his friends' reaction.

As she remained quiet, he was struck about how much Molly intrigued him in other ways. He still wasn't sure their meeting had been totally accidental, but she hadn't pushed to capture his interest like he expected. She was quietly confident in her own way.

She seemed content with her life the way it was going and hadn't once suggested they change their status from pretend to real.

In fact, she had not asked for a single thing from him.

Nick frowned. That couldn't be right. Everyone wanted something from him. But even offering to compensate her for her postponed weekend at some spa had been refused.

For the first time, Nick began to wonder if Molly was for real. If it wasn't some act she was playing, but the genuine article. Were there women who weren't out for the main chance?

It was still early for a Saturday evening, and parking was easy in front of Molly's building.

"I guess you're in a hurry to get home," she said when he stopped the car.

"Invite me in for coffee," he countered.

She looked at him in surprise, her gaze drifting to his mouth. "Just coffee?" she asked.

Nick opened the door and went to open hers. He was making no promises tonight. Molly looked like every man's fantasy in that dress with her hair up, begging to be undone and allowed to fall to her shoulders. Those same shoulders now covered by her coat, but which had been tempting him all evening.

When they entered the flat, she shrugged off her coat and draped it across a chair. She walked to the open kitchen and Nick watched her hips sway beneath the dress. He loosened his tie, and removed his jacket. It was suddenly too warm.

He followed her and leaned his hip against the counter, crossing his arms over his chest as she prepared the coffee. She glanced at him from time to time. Did she feel the same draw of attraction? Or was she merely wondering how soon she could get rid of him?

"You can wait in the living room," she said.

"Trying to get rid of me?"

She faced him and nodded emphatically. "Yes, you make me nervous."

Nick moved closer, crowding her until she was back against the sink. He placed a hand on either side of her and leaned closer.

"How nervous?"

"Very nervous," she said, her eyes challenging him, her whole body challenging him. He wanted Molly McGuire.

Her palm came to rest against his chest. He waited. Was she going to push him away? She didn't. The warmth of her hand seemed to burn through his shirt.

Slowly he leaned closer to kiss her. He hadn't tasted those lips since the kiss earlier at the ball. It had been hours. He wanted another taste.

"This isn't a good idea," she said in a throaty low voice even as her face tilted up to meet his.

With a soft sigh, Molly closed her eyes, and met his lips with hers.

It was a gentle kiss, sweet and tender. He held himself in check, letting her call the shots. She moved against him and he wrapped her in his arms, relishing the feel of her feminine body against his, the flowery scent of her that seemed to surround them. Her honeyed taste remembered.

The shrill whistle from the teakettle interrupted. Slowly he released her, already wanting more.

"Go on in the living room, I'll bring the coffee in a moment," she said.

Nick nodded and left the tiny kitchen. When he entered the high-ceilinged room, he remembered her telling his mother about her painting foray. He looked up. The walls were high. If she ever did it again, he hoped she'd hire a painter.

The bedroom loft had a half wall that gave privacy from the living room, but would enable Molly to look over if she chose. He wanted to climb the spiral stairs and see her bedroom. Did she have a large bed, or a single?

Turning away from the disturbing image of Molly in bed with someone else, he looked at the painting on the easel near the window. He crossed the room to study it. He didn't know the exact spot but he'd bet it was from the Japanese Tea Garden. She had captured it in early morning, with fog still drifting overhead, the serenity and peaceful setting reflected perfectly. He could almost feel the cool air, see the ripples in the water. He hadn't realized she was so talented.

"Do you take anything in your coffee?" she asked.

He turned but didn't move away from the painting. "Black. Do you have a buyer for this painting?"

She walked over and handed him a mug. She shook her head.

"Who handles your work?"

"I have some in a couple of galleries. Buchards on Market and Samuel's at the wharf."

He looked at the painting again. "I'll buy this one."

Molly sipped her tea and studied the painting. She looked at Nick with curiosity. ''Why?''

''What do you mean, why? It's a sale, isn't it?''

''I guess. I'm just surprised, that's all.''

He looked at the paintings that were hanging on the walls. Stepping around Molly, he went to study each of the three. One was a seascape, bold and daring. He could almost taste the salty air. The one near the chair and lamp was of an English country garden, lots of flowers, and so romance-y he knew it would appeal to women everywhere. The third one, near the bookcase was another of Golden Gate Park—of the grassy areas where families picnicked and children played.

''Why are you working at Zentech when you could make a fortune with the painting?'' he asked, turning to look at her.

''Zentech is bread and butter, the rest is jam,'' she said.

''So will you sell me the painting?''

''Sure. Do you want me to have it framed first?''

''Yes.''

She named a figure Nick thought ridiculously low, but he wasn't going to bargain up. If that was the price she set, so be it.

She went to the sofa and sat down, tucking her legs beneath her. Placing her cup on the coffee table, she looked at him.

''I read the fact sheet Donny prepared, before I went to see your mother, just in case. He didn't list any hobbies. Do you work all the time?''

He came to sit beside her, close enough to touch, but with space between them. Placing his cup beside hers, he leaned back against the cushions. "I don't have time for hobbies. Unless you count running. I try to get in a few hours a week. But Magellan's takes most of my time. Not just the one here, but all up and down the coast. Some weeks I feel I'm living in an airplane."

"Do you read when on the plane?"

"Sure, reports, spreadsheets, market analyses. Why the interest?"

"Just in case."

"In case?"

"I'm questioned about it around your mother. She'd think it odd if I didn't know more about you. She told me about your growing up, though come to think about it she didn't mention Mrs. Porter's Academy."

"That's classified information, don't you be spreading it around, either."

She laughed and Nick was lost.

He reached for her, gratified when she came willingly. A few kisses and he'd either take them up those spiral stairs, or leave before he got further involved.

But one kiss was all she gave. Then she pushed back, touched his cheek lightly and rose. "You need to go."

He stood beside her. "Or I could stay." His hand encircled her neck, urging her closer. But Molly stood firm.

"No, you can't stay. Nick, this is a pretend engagement, entered into solely to help your mother. And I'm not the type to sleep around."

"But you think I am?"

"Carmen could answer that for us."

He shook her gently, then released her. "I may have had an affair or two in the past. At my age, did you expect me to be a monk?

"I don't expect anything from you—except for you to leave now."

"What are you doing tomorrow?" he asked as he went to pick up his jacket.

"Errands, and chores, why?"

"Chores?"

"Vacuum this place, do laundry, I don't know, whatever needs to be done."

"Spend the day with me," he said. "When my mother asks, you don't want me to lie, do you?"

Molly laughed. "This whole charade is a lie. What's one more."

"Spend the day with me."

"Doing what?" Molly knew she shouldn't but temptation was strong. She would like to see more of him before they called a halt to their engagement. And if his mother continued to recover as fast as she seemed to be, the need for their engagement would end soon. Long before her own parents returned.

"Whatever you want."

"Oh wow, that's tempting."

"Within reason," he added hastily.

"How long since you've ridden a cable car?"

"What?"

She smiled. "Okay, here's the deal, we meet at the top of Lombard Street and walk down the crooked part then head for the wharf. We can ramble around there for a while, even check out Pier 39. Then take a cable car to Chinatown and have dim sum for lunch. Are the Giants playing? We could go to the stadium and watch a ball game. I'm not crazy about football, but don't mind baseball. It's going to be gorgeous tomorrow.''

''Sounds like a tourist outing, hit all the high spots of the city.''

''So why should tourists have all the fun. We live here, we should enjoy the high spots ourselves!''

''Ten o'clock?''

''At the top of Lombard.''

He nodded and left.

Molly stared at the door for a long moment, bemused by his agreeing. She hadn't expected that. Would he enjoy the day?

She hoped so. If nothing else, it could provide a shared memory she could take out and enjoy in the years ahead.

CHAPTER EIGHT

PROMPTLY at ten, Molly reached the top of the hill where Lombard began its crooked descent. The hydrangea hugging each curve were in full bloom, their pink and blue snowball blossoms adding color to the already picturesque block.

She'd worn her hair tied back, to keep it out of her face in the ocean breeze. The jeans and a shirt covered with a sweater were casual. She wondered what Nick would wear. Maybe those running shorts.

She grinned at the thought and watched as people began the descent by car, slowly maneuvering the tight hairpin turns.

Tourists walked down the steps, some stopping to take a photograph of the many blossoms.

She glanced at her watch. She'd thought Nick was always punctual. It was two minutes after ten—

"Parking is a bear around here," he said behind her.

When Molly turned, Nick leaned over and kissed her as if it was the most natural thing in the world.

"I took the cable car, didn't have to worry about parking."

"Do you even own a car?"

She shook her head. "Why bother when public transportation is so easy. Ready?"

"Lead on, McDuff." He threaded his fingers through hers and they began their Sunday together.

Molly held his hand, loving the feel of his warm palm against hers. Loving the pretense of being a couple, out to make happy memories and enjoy the time they spent together.

Justin had never made the effort, and they'd been dating. But except when Molly really put her foot down, all their time together had been about Justin. How had she convinced herself she cared anything about the man?

Nick and she were practically strangers, knew they had nothing in common and a limited time together. Yet he was a lot more open about doing things than Justin. Was it because they weren't really a couple? Or was Nick just a different kind of man?

"You didn't object when I suggested dim sum for lunch, you like Chinese food?"

"With Shu-Wen as our cook, what do you think? She's been with mother for years and often prepared Chinese. As a kid there was a time when I loved to spend afternoons in the kitchen, watching her prepare sui mai or potstickers. She'd always have to test one or two—so I'd get an early start on dinner."

"I love it myself. I'd eat dim sum for lunch every day if I could. But most of my friends at work don't care that much for it. So once or twice a month is our limit."

"Do you also like Japanese?"

They discussed food likes and dislikes as they walked along. Soon Lombard Street was behind them and they were heading for Fisherman's Wharf. As they descended the steep hills, the blue bay lay before them. Whitecaps dusted the water from the brisk ocean breeze. Molly felt warm as toast in her sweater, with her hand held in Nick's. She had no trouble keeping up with him, but he wasn't strolling.

From food they moved on to discussing architecture, using examples of the places they passed as to what was appealing and what was functional.

Mingling with the crowd later on the wharf, Molly was charmed by the way Nick protected her, drawing her out of the way of a bunch of rowdy teenagers, sheltering her from being jostled at a crosswalk. And keeping the street vendors from becoming a nuisance with one look.

She wished she could capture that look.

In fact, she wished she could capture the entire day! She was enjoying herself far more than she'd expected. And all because Nick was so much fun to be with.

Gone was the suspicious hotel mogul. Instead, he was just a man, and she was just a woman, both bent on having a great day together.

But it's still make-believe, she reminded herself. They would never have met had she not wandered into the bar at the Magellan Hotel and poured her woes on the bartender.

When they passed Samuel's Galleries, Nick stopped and went back, pulling Molly with him.

"Isn't this one of the galleries that carry your work?" he asked.

"Yes." She was surprised he remembered. Before she could say anything else, he led them inside.

"Show me," he said.

Molly pointed to the left where several of her paintings were displayed. They wandered over and she watched Nick as he studied each one. His impassive expression gave nothing away and she was on tenterhooks wondering if he liked the work or was trying to find a way to be polite.

He looked at her. ''They're good.''

''Thank you.''

''I especially like the sailboats.''

She smiled. ''I do, too, actually. It took a lot of tries to get the sea just right.''

A discreet salesman hovered nearby. Nick caught his eye and the man came promptly over.

''May I assist in any way?'' he asked.

Nick withdrew his wallet and pulled out a business card, handing it to the salesman. ''I'm interested in purchasing these paintings,'' he said, gesturing to the wall which held Molly's pictures.

The man blinked, read the card and then looked at Nick. ''All of them?''

''All the ones by Molly McGuire.''

''What? Nick are you crazy? You can't buy all the paintings,'' Molly protested, astonished he'd even suggest the idea.

''I have eight luxury hotels. We decorate with top quality artwork, why can't I add these paintings to our collection?''

Molly didn't know what to say. There were seven paintings. It had taken her more than two years to paint them. Was he serious about buying them all for his hotels?

She tried to see the angle, wasn't he always doing that? Why he would spend so much money on paintings just because he knew the artist? There had to be a hidden agenda she was unaware of.

The salesman looked from one to the other, obviously unsure how to proceed. Molly almost smiled at his confusion. She could certainly empathize. He probably had never had anyone buy seven paintings at one time—especially with the prices Samuel's had given them.

"I'll have the addresses sent tomorrow for you to ship. I don't want them all at one hotel. Will your firm send an invoice?"

The man cleared his throat. "Would you excuse me for a moment. I'm not sure how we'll handle this." He quickly headed for the back of the gallery.

Nick studied the paintings again.

"You don't have to do this," she said.

"Of course I don't," he said arrogantly. "But I'd be a fool to pass up good work when I see it. Besides, I expect the investment will grow in value."

Molly felt a warm glow spread through her. This tough businessman was buying her work because he thought it would increase in value. It was the nicest compliment she'd ever received!

"Ah, Molly, my dear," Harold Samuel came from the back, trailed by the salesman. "How nice to see you again. And Mr. Bailey, I'm honored to have you visit our gallery." He beamed at them both, turning his gaze to Molly. "And congratulations are in order, I believe. I saw the article in the newspaper about your engagement."

She smiled and stifled a groan. Had the entire world seen that newspaper article?

"We are happy to crate and ship the paintings wherever you wish, Mr. Bailey," he said to Nick. "If it is convenient, just have the addresses faxed to us tomorrow. We'll have them shipped by Wednesday."

He motioned the salesman forward. "Molly is the artist. And this is her fiancé. A romantic gesture of the highest order—buying her collection to place in your hotels. You won't regret it. Molly does marvelous work."

"I think so," Nick said.

"But you have taken my entire inventory of her work." He shook his head and looked at Molly. "When may I expect more?"

"Soon. The piece I just finished has already been sold," she said, flicking Nick another glance.

"That one is for my personal collection," Nick said.

"I understand. I do hope we may represent more of your work in the future," Harold said genially.

They spoke a few moments longer then Nick and Molly left, Molly still reeling from the transaction.

"I don't know what to say," she murmured as they continued walking along the wharf, dodging tourists, watching kites in the distance dancing on the breeze. The total amount for seven paintings was staggering. She'd thought the gallery had overpriced them when they were first hung. Nick hadn't even haggled. Maybe Harold knew what he was doing!

"Want to go with me to select the right spot in each hotel where they can hang?" Nick asked.

She eyed him uncertainly. Was he joking? Most likely. The head of the corporation didn't place paintings. He had dozens of minions for those kinds of tasks.

Molly shrugged and didn't respond. No sense letting him know how much she'd love to see her paintings in the lobbies of Magellan's Hotels. Maybe she'd check out the one on Union Square in a week or so, to see if there was truly one of her painting on display.

"Getting hungry?" Nick asked.

"Yes." The fresh air and sunshine had sparked her appetite. It seemed like forever since she'd had breakfast.

They decided to walk to Chinatown, noticing how the buildings changed from the newer ones near the wharf to older buildings as they approached Little Italy at Washington Square. Molly glanced at the restaurant they'd eaten in a few nights ago as they walked past. She already had memories shared with Nick.

Soon they turned onto Grant Avenue where Molly always felt as if she'd taken a side trip to Taiwan. The aromas emanating from the restaurants were heavenly. And the old women carrying shopping bags, walking bent over with the weight of small grandbabies tied on their backs emphasizing a culture so different from her own which flourished in San Francisco.

He led the way to a restaurant known for its excellence. Entering, Molly was bemused to notice they were the only non-Asian customers in the place.

"It's wonderful in here," she said as the hostess promptly seated them.

"Best dim sum in town."

As the carts rumbled by and Nick selected for them, Molly was content to watch. He'd ask if she wanted a dish and she was willing to try them all—even the ones she didn't recognize. He ordered in

Chinese, not just pointing to the plates on the tray. Shu-Wen's influence, she knew.

"Delicious," she pronounced taking her first bite. "Does Shu-Wen ever make dim sum?"

"Occasionally. Mom would have a luncheon for her Garden Club and as a special treat Shu-Wen would prepare dim sum, but it's a lot of work to have this variety for a small group."

Just then Nick's cell phone rang. He excused himself and flipped it open.

"Bailey."

Molly took another bite and gazed around, trying not to eavesdrop on his conversation, which was impossible since he was so close.

"Yes, as a matter of fact, she's right here."

She looked over at that.

He held out the phone. "It's for you."

"Me?" She took it and said hello.

"Molly, dear, I suspected you two would be together. It's good to know Nick is taking some time off from work to spend with you. I enjoyed our lunch yesterday," Ellen Bailey said warmly.

"I did, too."

"What's that noise in the background?"

"We're at a restaurant having lunch," Molly replied.

"Oh dear, bad timing. I won't keep you, dear. I just wanted to see if you are free on next Saturday evening. I thought I'd have a small group of family friends in to meet you. It wouldn't be a formal engagement party, I know you'll want to wait for your parents to return for that. But I'm dying to show you off to my friends."

Molly looked at Nick. Some of her consternation must have shown, because he took the phone from her.

"What's going on, Mom?"

Molly watched as his expression darkened. "No, don't do that. You need to rest up and get better before entertaining."

He was quiet a moment, then took a deep breath. "Mom, can we discuss this later? ... No." He flicked Molly a glance. "Actually, we had made plans to visit some of the other hotels. We'll be gone all weekend."

Molly felt her breath catch. The two of them going off for a weekend? She didn't think so. He was using it only as an excuse to fob off his mother. While planning for a future event seemed to be acting as a tonic, a party seemed excessive right now. But so did Nick's excuse!

He flipped the cell phone closed a moment later and slipped it back into his pocket.

"This is getting out of hand," he said.

"Maybe, but it also seems to be working. She's feeling lots better, isn't she?" Molly asked.

"She would be overdoing it if she hosted a party this weekend, no matter how few and close the friends. Anyway, I told her we wouldn't be in town."

"I heard." Molly cleared her throat. "As an excuse, it sounds good."

He raised an eyebrow. "Sounds good?"

"I mean, if she thinks we're out of town, that's as good as being out of town, right?"

"I meant it. We'll fly down to L.A. or San Diego and stay at the hotel there."

Molly opened her mouth to protest, "You may be

used to ordering your employees around, but I don't take orders from you."

"What?"

"Maybe I have plans next weekend."

"Do you?"

Her mind went blank. Surely there was something she could claim. "I'd have to check my calendar."

"Come on, Molly. There's nothing that can't wait. You already canceled your visit to the spa. Let me make that up to you with a trip to our San Diego hotel. It's really special—right on Mission Bay, with catamarans and paddle wheel boats, miles of sugar beaches and dining to delight all the senses."

She grinned. "You sound like a commercial."

"Hey, I'm proud of our hotels. Especially that one."

"Why that one?"

"It's mine from start to finish. I acquired it after my father died, built its reputation by some innovative ideas. It's one of the most popular in the chain."

He stopped a cart to order har gow and shu mai. Molly was beginning to feel full, but the food was so delicious she didn't want to stop.

She ate thoughtfully, still hearing the ring of pride when Nick spoke of the San Diego hotel.

"Did good business dictate you buy the hotel in San Diego?" she asked.

He shook his head. "It was a gamble. The hotels my dad had managed were doing well, but not spectacularly so. Money was a little tight and I went out on a limb to finance the acquisition. But I wanted a hotel in that market and when one became available, I snapped it up."

"Risky."

"Of course, but if you want something enough, it's worth any risk."

"And why did you—want it I mean? Wasn't what you had enough?"

"It would have been, but it was my dad's and grandfather's before him. I wanted something to prove I could make a difference. And I needed something to show the staffing at all the hotels I knew what I was doing when I proposed change. That I could lead the company in a new direction and have it flourish."

"You succeeded." Magellan Hotels were world famous.

He nodded calmly and placed another dumpling on his plate.

"Was it scary?" she asked.

"Challenging," he replied.

Men looked at things differently, she knew. But it took guts and determination and a lot of confidence to put an existing company in jeopardy to go forth with a new and risky venture. She was glad it had turned out well for him.

"So are you coming to see my baby?" he asked.

"We could just pretend we went away. If neither of us answers our phones all weekend, your mother would never know we were in town. It's not as if she's likely to go out and spy on us."

"I'd like you to come."

She hadn't expected that. "Why?"

"To see it. You missed your spa trip, let me make it up to you for helping me out."

"You did that by buying seven paintings." She

shook her head, still astonished he'd have done such a thing.

"The sailing one will be perfect in the lobby in San Diego. Come with me Molly and see it there."

His phone rang again.

"Dammit, can't a man have a day off?" he grumbled as he flipped it open again.

"Bailey."

Molly was glad for the interruption. She couldn't imagine herself taking off for a weekend with Nick. Would he expect more than studying how the picture looked in the lobby? She almost laughed, of course he would, he was a man, wasn't he?

Even if their relationship had been different, Molly wasn't the type to go off on weekends with men. And their relationship was not as they were pretending.

But if she could establish some guidelines, dare she take the opportunity? She hadn't ever stayed in a Magellan Hotel, probably wouldn't in the future, they were too expensive. Why not indulge herself—as long as they both knew going in it would be strictly platonic.

"I'll be right there."

Nick's words penetrated her thoughts. She watched as he flipped the phone closed.

"I have to go." He raised his hand, quickly summoning the waitress for the tally and bill.

Molly gulped down the rest of her tea and wrapped the custard desserts in a napkin. "What's up? Is it your mother?" Had something happened to her in the interval between the first and second call?

"No, Donny's holding someone he thinks is the

one skimming money from the bar. Before we call the cops, I want to talk to him.''

It was only a few blocks from the restaurant to Union Square, and Nick set a fast pace.

''Shouldn't you let the cops interrogate him?'' she said breathlessly, trying to keep up.

''They will, I want first crack. It's my hotel he's ripping off.'' The implacable tone made Molly glad he was not angry with her!

When they reached the hotel, Nick went straight to the elevators. When one arrived, it was empty. They stepped in and Nick pushed button thirteen.

''The hotel's offices are on the thirteenth floor?'' Molly asked. If she'd been asked, she would have thought they would take the top floor—for the view.

''Some guests are superstitious. This way, no one has to stay on the thirteenth floor. And the view is almost as good as at the top,'' Nick explained, but from the leashed energy she knew the answer was absently given, his focus was on what Donny had told him.

The offices were beautifully decorated, pale gray walls with original artwork displayed tastefully. The deep burgundy carpet was thick beneath her feet. At Zentech plush offices were only for the most senior staff members. Even entry-level clerks enjoyed Magellan's plush design.

Nick headed away from the elevators, a moment later pushed open a door and entered the office.

Molly paused at the doorway and studied the lay-out. Donny stood near the window. Gone was the genial bartender. Instead, he looked as dangerous as Nick. They both glared at the man in the chair in front of the desk. He was squirming in the seat, obviously nervous and trying to put on a brave face, but intimidated by the two men towering over him.

"I'll just wait out here," Molly murmured. Stepping back, she pulled the door closed. Sitting near the secretary's desk, she opened the napkin she'd carefully carried and began to nibble on a custard tart.

Being with Nick was certainly never boring. He intrigued her more and more each time they were together. He could be fun and act carefree, but she knew it was an act. Always beneath the surface he was focused on his priorities. And his business was at the top of the list.

On the other hand, she mused, listening for any sounds from the office, one always knew exactly where he or she stood with Nick. So far she had not seen any signs of manipulation or currying favors like Justin had displayed.

She frowned, wishing she had not thought about Justin. Her own judgment was at fault there. How could she have thought he cared for her—or that she loved him?

She knew—Molly's brain almost stopped functioning.

No. She was not going to say she knew the difference. She didn't know anything. She was *not* going there. She did not, could not, would not love Nick Bailey!

They had nothing in common. Except for the man in the office who had stolen from the bar, they would never even have met.

So they entered a temporary arrangement to hasten

Ellen's recovery. Didn't mean they even had to be friends.

She was not falling in love with Nick!

Molly rose, glanced at the door, and made her decision. He would never miss her. And she had to get a life. Something away from the disturbing influence of Nick. And away from the thoughts that plagued.

She pulled a sheet of paper from the nearby printer and scribbled a hasty note. Leaving it where Nick would be sure to see it, she took off like a shot. She was playing with fire to stay around Nick. Once she'd served her purpose, she'd be out of his life so fast her head would spin. It would be totally crazy to develop any feelings for the man.

But even as she descended in the elevator, she feared it was too late.

Molly stepped out into the sunshine. But the joy in the day had faded with the worry she had done something so stupid as to fall for the man.

Turning right, she began to walk. Maybe the fresh air would clear her head of foolishness.

But as the blocks fell behind her, her mind didn't clear, but constantly remembered every moment she'd spent with Nick, from dancing in his arms last night, to the first time she'd met him, to the kisses they'd shared.

Molly was startled when she looked up and realized she was home. She lived miles from Union Square. She stormed inside and went to Shelly's door, ringing the bell impatiently.

Shelly opened, looking at her in surprise.

"Hi, Molly, thought you were going out with the hunk today."

Molly walked past her friend and paced into the middle of her living room. "I am so mad I could spit!" she said.

"Whoa, date not go well?" Shelly closed the door and watched Molly pace in agitation.

Molly waved her hand. "It went fine, until the thief was caught and I think I'm falling for the blasted man!"

"You're falling for a thief?"

"No—Nick Bailey."

Shelly smiled. "So what's the problem. I told you it was as easy to fall for a rich man as a poor one. Think what fun you can have spending the night in a different hotel whenever you want!"

"I don't care a bit about staying in hotels. I have a perfectly wonderful flat right in this building."

"Which you won't stay in if you marry Nick. I suspect he wouldn't want to live down here."

"Marriage? There is nothing like marriage between us. You know his agenda in this whole pretense. Once his mother is fully recovered, it's sayonara Molly."

"Maybe not, he seemed to like you when he picked you up. Has he ever kissed you?"

Molly shrugged. "Maybe once or twice. But it meant nothing. I kissed Justin, and that went exactly nowhere, too."

"I wouldn't put Nick and Justin in the same sentence," Shelly commented dryly. "They are nothing alike."

"They are, too," Molly stated firmly, trying to convince herself. "They are both men with their own agendas."

"No. Justin set out to feather his own nest. Nick

was coerced into the situation, and only asked you to continue when he saw the benefit to someone else—his mother.''

Molly stopped pacing and looked at her friend. ''What am I going to do?'

''Enjoy?''

''It hurt my feelings when Justin dumped me so unceremoniously. But this is much bigger, Shelly. We're talking about my heart here.''

Shelly went to give Molly a quick hug. She gestured to the sofa, ''Sit down and let's talk about it. Maybe you can make him fall in love with you.''

''Oh, yeah, I have a life-size picture of that ever happening. You haven't seen Carmen—the kind of woman he usually dates. Trust me, falling in love with me is not an option. I have to stop seeing him now. I could be imagining all this, don't you think? It could just be wishful thinking as a reaction to Justin's dumping me and all.''

''Sure. Out of sight, out of mind. You can stay away from him all week with work and all. Then next weekend take that time off for the spa like you planned before. By then his mother will be fully recovered and you're off the hook!''

Molly nodded, trying to garner enthusiasm for Shelly's suggestions. She could take her postponed trip, but she couldn't help thinking about a weekend in a Magellan Hotel in San Diego.

''He bought all my paintings,'' she said slowly.

''What?''

''We went to the wharf, and he remembered Samuel's Gallery had some of my paintings on display. We went in to see them and he bought them all.''

Shelly stared at her. ''You're kidding?''

''No. He never even haggled. He told me he wanted the one I just finished, as well.''

''Oh, wow.'' Shelly's eyes were wide as she considered this bit of news.

Molly nodded. ''Oh, wow, is right.''

''It's such a romantic gesture.''

''No, just business. They have lovely paintings in the hotels, original art. He's planning to add my work to the hotels' collection. Except the one I just finished, which he said was for his personal collection.''

''Maybe you should give him the benefit of the doubt,'' Shelly suggested slowly. ''Maybe we're calling this wrong. I never heard of anyone buying a collection of work from a relatively unknown artist like that.''

''I don't think there is any doubt. I saw how ruthless he's been with Carmen. And you should have seen him when he walked in on the thief—no mercy at all. I don't want to be at the receiving end of that. If I cut loose now, I can get over him quickly—maybe I'm just romanticizing the entire thing. We did have fun this morning, so I could be fantasizing more about what might have been instead of reality.''

''I'm not following you,'' Shelly said, perplexed.

Molly jumped up. ''I'm not, either. I think I'll go home and have some chocolate and figure out how to stop thinking about Nick Bailey.''

Shelly rose as well and followed Molly to the door. ''Or give yourselves a chance. You're a terrific person, Molly, I don't see why he wouldn't fall head over heels for you.''

Molly hugged her. "You're a true friend. Want to go to a movie one night this week? I'll have a lot of free time.''

''So you really aren't going to see him anymore?''

''I don't think it's very smart if I do. What's the point? He can tell his mother we are seeing each other. Make up something about my being too busy to visit. She'll get better in a short while, and he can tell her we drifted apart.'' She smiled, hoping the bleakness that enveloped her heart wasn't showing. With a half wave, she headed for her own flat.

But despite her brave words, tears trembled in her eyes. Her heart ached like it had been punched. She was falling for the man. What a mess. Trying to get out of one situation plunged her into a worse one. One, moreover, she suspected it would take her a long time to recover from.

Alone in her flat, she walked to the picture, dashing away the tears. He liked her work. He wanted this picture for his personal collection.

When he looked at it, would he think of the artist who had painted it? Or only see the cool morning in Golden Gate Park?

The phone rang. Molly ignored it. She listened to the answering machine when it clicked on.

''Molly? It's Nick, are you home?'' The silence ticked by. ''Call me when you get home,'' he said before hanging up.

She walked over and replayed the message, listening to his voice. Then she deliberately erased it. She was not going to moon over the man like some teenager with a crush.

Turning, she took the picture off the easel. Tomorrow, she'd take it to have it framed and then crated for shipment. And that would be that.

CHAPTER NINE

BY WEDNESDAY, Molly began to think she should have confronted Nick and explained she wanted out of their agreement. He'd helped her out for one evening. Surely all the pretending she had done squared the account.

By Tuesday, she unplugged her answering machine—there were too many messages from Nick to keep it plugged in. Seeing the flashing light when she'd walked in, she hadn't listened to him, but erased them all.

Maybe she'd send him a note. That way she wouldn't have to see him again, but would make it clear they were through and it was up to him to concoct some story for Ellen as to why they were no longer engaged.

And the sooner the better. She spent more time thinking about him than attending to work. She'd been studying this layout for ten minutes and couldn't even remember what it was for.

Suddenly a feeling of disquiet came over her. She looked up. Nick was crossing through the open area as if he owned Zentech. No, come to think of it, the owners didn't stride through so arrogantly.

She put down her pencil and braced herself. He looked as dashing as ever, and much the angry pirate. His gaze snared hers and she couldn't look away.

Maybe she should have answered at least one of the phone calls.

"Your answering machine is broken," he said without any greeting. He stopped by her desk and glared at her. "Or you are ignoring my calls."

"Why would I do that?" she asked, licking suddenly dry lips.

"Good question, one I don't have an answer for. I've been trying to reach you since Sunday. Why did you leave so abruptly?"

"I didn't know how long you'd be, questioning your suspect. Was he guilty? Was he the one who pilfered the money?"

"He was. He's in police custody now, and a quiet warning has spread throughout the entire chain I won't tolerate theft."

"So Donny's days as bartender are over?"

He nodded, his eyes narrowed slightly. Flicking a glance at his watch, he said, "It's almost lunchtime, get your things, I'll treat."

Molly knew she should refuse, even opened her mouth to do so, when Justin strolled into view. He was finally working with Nathan on the delayed artwork, but he kept looking over toward Molly.

Pasting a brilliant smile on her face, she gazed lovingly at Nick. "How wonderful, darling, I'd love to." She covered the work on her drafting table, slid off the high stool and grabbed her purse. "It'll have to be casual, I'm not dressed for a fancy place." She slipped her hand into the crook of Nick's arm and almost batted her eyelashes at him.

A jaw muscle tightened in his face. "So glad, *darling,* that you can spare the time."

"I always have time for you, Nicky," she said, louder than needed. She wanted to make sure Justin got the message—she and Nick were still an item!

As they turned, Nick spotted Justin. He nodded once in the man's direction, then looked straight ahead.

"What's going on, Molly? Ignore me until you need reinforcements, then latch on to fool the opposition?"

"The opposition?"

"Justin?"

"Nick, you invited me to lunch. We're engaged, after all, why wouldn't I be delighted to see my fiancé?"

"You tell me first why you've ignored every message I've left."

She stalled for time, until they were in the elevator, when she dropped the adoring pose like a hot potato. The two other occupants in the elevator made conversation impossible. She'd wait until they had some semblance of privacy.

The busy sidewalk provided it. "I've been busy this week," she said as they walked toward Market Street.

"Too busy to call and say, I'm busy?" he asked. "To busy to return my mother's calls?"

"Your mother called?" She hadn't listened to the messages after the first day, suspecting they all were from Nick. "I didn't know."

"She wanted an answer to her proposal for a small dinner party this weekend."

"I'm going off."

"So I told her. That we would be going to San Diego to supervise the placement of your paintings."

Molly stopped. Ignoring the people who jostled her as they hurried by, she stared at him. "You did what?"

He took her arm, urging her along the crowded sidewalk. "We discussed it on Sunday, surely it didn't slip your mind."

"You suggested it. I never said I'd go."

"I made reservations for an early flight Saturday morning. We'll be home Sunday night."

"Of all the nerve. Nick, I'm not going off with you for a weekend. This is a fake engagement, remember?"

"Is that what has you worried? I booked a suite, two bedrooms. Your virtue is safe with me, Molly."

"No, that's not what has me worried." She closed her mouth suddenly, realizing what she had been about to say. The last thing she wanted was for him to have even a glimmer of an idea that her feelings had undergone a change. Instead of a business deal, she'd give her back teeth to have it change into a romantic affair.

Wouldn't he get a kick out of that bit of news.

"Then what?"

"I'm going to the spa this weekend. The one I was going to before." She sounded almost petulant in stating the fact.

"Another time. Come with me to San Diego."

His voice was compelling, making her wish for things that could never be. Intoxicating, like sparkling wine along her senses, awakening her to awareness and needs that were new and exciting.

She glanced up, and saw the intensity of his gaze. His dark eyes seemed to see through to her soul.

''Have you ever been to San Diego?''

She shook her head, mesmerized by the look in his eyes.

''I've heard it's lovely,'' she said.

''Mission Bay is especially enchanting, and the Magellan Hotel there was designed to enhance the enchantment. Say you'll come.''

Molly looked away, trying to remember why she wanted to keep her distance. Surely a weekend wouldn't hurt—and it would give her a chance to see San Diego, see her paintings in the lobby of a famous hotel.

Give her a weekend with Nick.

See him in his element, the lordly hotel owner, showing off one of his hotels. Maybe she'd get disgusted with him and be able to easily say goodbye on Sunday night.

Reasoning took hold. ''I can't go.''

''It's that or the party at my mother's,'' he said shortly.

''No, it's not. Tell your mother we're going off, then just stay home and don't answer the phone.''

''Like you've been doing all week?'' he asked silkily.

''I've been busy,'' she protested, unwilling to concede defeat.

Nick paused by a doorway and ushered Molly inside a small sandwich shop. They joined the line waiting to order and she glanced around, recognizing one other person from work. The place was one she ate in often, and she knew was a favorite with many from

Zentech. When her coworker waved, Molly acknowledged her and turned back to Nick, hoping she looked like she was enjoying herself, and not provoked. If she ended things with Nick, would there be talk at work? She was tired of being the main fodder for the gossip mill.

"Friend of yours?" he asked.

"Someone from work." She stepped up and ordered, then waited while Nick ordered and paid for both sandwiches and drinks. They moved down the counter to wait for them to be prepared.

"Shall we eat outside?" Molly asked, not wanting to have a conversation in such a crowded place. Who knew who might be listening?

"It's a short walk to the Embarcadero. We can go there, if you like."

He was being accommodating, nice. She wished he would be as arrogant as he could get sometimes. It would make things easier.

Before long they were sitting on a bench in a quiet little park, dappled sunshine giving them respite from the sun. The breeze was slight, cool and refreshing.

Molly took a bite of her sandwich and looked at Nick.

"Now's when you bring in the heavy guns," she said.

"Meaning?"

"What threats are you going to use to make me go to San Diego."

A gleam of amusement lit his eyes. "Threats? Wouldn't a simple invitation do?"

She shook her head warily. "I don't want to go."

''Do you not want to go, or not want to go with me?''

That gave her pause. ''With you.''

''I told you, you have nothing to worry about.''

''Just being with you makes me worry,'' she blurted.

''Ah, and that is because?''

She took another bite, unwilling to say anything more. Her tummy felt fluttery, her skin tingly and her heart raced. Just being with Nick. What would it be like to spend a weekend together? They'd get the best service, of that she was sure. And San Diego, renowned for its sparkling beaches, casual attitude and warm weather—outstanding even in California.

She'd never get such an opportunity again.

And get to see her painting put on display in the lobby.

And get to spend a few more days with Nick Bailey.

A wise woman would run in the opposite direction. Molly looked at him again, and jumped in with both feet. ''Okay, early Saturday morning we leave for San Diego. How is your mother?''

''Recovering remarkably well.''

''So we don't need to continue this charade much longer?''

Nick shrugged, for some reason unwilling to give Molly a date when they could end the charade as she put it. His mother's health was recovering quickly. He'd spoken with her doctor yesterday and been told the man was confident she'd regain her lost strength in a short while and be as fit as could be in no time.

Nick knew better than to believe his mother would go into a decline when he told her he and Molly were no longer engaged, but he didn't want any setbacks, either. It wouldn't hurt to continue a little longer.

"You don't have anyone in the wings, do you?" he asked.

"What wings?"

"It's an expression. Is there someone you'd rather be seeing?"

"Of course not. After Justin's trick, do you think I want to rush back into the dating scene? Not likely."

"Then what's the rush to end our arrangement?"

He watched her expression, wishing he could read minds. What was going on in that head?

He found a lot of benefit to the arrangement—Carmen had stopped calling, his mother was recovering, and he had an escort to social events, one with no expectations, and who wasn't constantly trying to impress him.

There was more to this than he'd originally expected. Maybe he should have thought to enter an engagement-of-convenience a long time ago. Found someone who was content to remain single, yet wanted someone to do things with occasionally.

"Actually, I'm in no rush to end the engagement," he said slowly, testing the waters.

"You're kidding?" Molly looked at him in surprise. "Why not?"

"Why would either of us? We have built-in protection against others, someone to do things with on occasion, and no strings attached."

She looked away, finishing the last of her sandwich and balling the wrapping paper into a tight wad.

"I can see the appeal to a man who doesn't want to get involved. But I do, at some point. Just not with someone like Justin. One day I want to get married, have some children, a dog. And have someone to grow old with.''

Nick frowned, not liking the image of Molly growing old with anyone. She was vibrant, young and beautiful. He could see her with children—knew her eyes would light up with delight. She'd be carefree and fun, and bring joy to each child she had.

He focused on the water, trying to forget that picture. But the image wouldn't leave.

''No one is saying you can't have that. But are you ready to do it now?'' he asked.

''Now, later, who knows when a person meets love.''

''Love is an overrated, romantic notion given by women to pretty up the basic instincts all humans have to mate.''

''Cynic,'' she teased.

''Dreamer,'' he retorted.

''Artists are allowed,'' she said, rising. ''Okay, you've accomplished your goal, we're going to San Diego. I need to get back to work. I'll see you Saturday. Should I meet you at the airport?''

''Oh no,'' he said, rising, as well. ''I wouldn't risk it. You might discover you're too busy. I'll pick you up at six.''

''In the morning? On a Saturday? That's my day to sleep in.''

''We have an eight o'clock flight. You don't want to waste the day. We can be on the beach in San Diego before lunchtime.''

Molly was not used to such casual travel. She rarely went on vacation beyond camping in Yosemite.

The thought of flying to San Diego to be lying on the beach by noon was fascinating.

As they ambled from the park, Molly dropped her trash in a container. Nick had achieved his goal—she was going away with him this weekend. How had that happened?

A lot could happen in a weekend.

Molly was enchanted with San Diego, just as Nick had predicted. The sugar-white sandy beaches beckoned, even when viewed from the airplane. The air was warmer, softer, than the crisp breezes she was used to in San Francisco. Palm trees swayed along boulevards as they took the hotel's limo to the hotel. Colorful bougainvillea covered walls and arched over doorways, deep red, bright purple, adding to the festive mood.

When they arrived at Magellan's San Diego, they were treated like royalty. Of course the staff knew Nick. He probably got that treatment everywhere—took it as a matter of course. But Molly was delighted with the warm welcome, and the fruit basket displayed prominently in the suite. She touched the cellophane wrapping lightly on her way to the large window. It overlooked the beach, in the quiet shelter of Mission Bay. Dozens of families were already enjoying the sun and cool water. The sparkling blue water was alluring.

Nick stood by the doorway to the suite, watching her, his hands in his pockets. "Want to go swimming?"

She turned, a bright smile hiding nothing.

"I sure do. It won't take me long to change once our suitcases arrive. This is a lovely hotel."

"Let's eat first, then we can spend the entire afternoon at the beach if you like. Later we can wander around the lobby and you can decide where to hang the painting. I selected the sailboats for this hotel."

She nodded, turning back to look at the water. They had a little more than twenty-four hours before the return flight, she wanted to make the most of every minute.

Once their bags arrived, Molly changed into her swimsuit, and then donned a loose sundress over it. Slipping on sandals, she pulled her hair up on her head, so it wouldn't get into her eyes once wet.

Going back to the sitting room of the suite, she waited for Nick, wandering around the luxurious room, admiring the furnishings, and the sense of elegance in every selection.

"Ready?" Nick asked from the door to his room. He was wearing shorts and a cotton shirt which was partially unbuttoned. She had the strongest urge to slip her fingertips into the opening and feel the warmth of his skin, test the strength of his muscles.

"Ready!" She turned toward the door, trying to get her thoughts under control. She had stipulated nothing physical between them, she couldn't change the rules to suit herself.

Nick led her to an outdoor café to one side of the huge hotel. Shaded by trees and strategically placed umbrellas, the tables provided a view of Mission Bay. Containers of bright flowers dotted the space, enhancing the feeling of dining in a tropical paradise.

"I have to have the shrimp salad," Molly said after

perusing the menu. ''It's the only thing that would fit this setting. It's so pretty here. How do you stay away? I'm itching to paint—'' She swept her hand in an arc, encompassing the entire setting. She would love to capture the different shades of blue that shimmered in the water, the reds and yellows of the flowers, the dark green of the trees. This was a feast for her senses.

''So come back sometime and paint it,'' Nick said casually. His eyes were hidden behind dark glasses. Molly wondered what he was thinking—maybe they'd come back together sometime? Or was he counting the days until his mother recovered and he no longer needed a fiancée-of-convenience.

When lunch was finished, they moved to the beach. It was crowded with families and couples, but walking along, they found a couple of empty reclining chairs and spread the towels the hotel had provided.

When Nick pulled off his shirt, Molly tried to keep her eyes on the water, but the pull of attraction was too strong. His skin was a warm honey color—not darkly tanned, but darker than her own. Obviously he took a few hours to swim in the sun during his visits to this hotel.

His bathing suit was tight, clearly defining his excellent physique. She swallowed, remembering how those muscles had felt when pressed against her. She had to get to the water to cool off—before she said or did something extremely foolish.

Slipping out of the dress, she almost ran to the edge of the bay. Molly stepped in, finding the water cool and refreshing. Soon she plunged in all the way, cooling her heated skin and trying to focus on anything but Nick Bailey.

But it wasn't easy when he joined her a second later, diving deep and then coming up beside her.

"This is nice," she said treading water, looking around. Time and again her gaze was drawn back to his. Daringly, she reached out and touched his shoulder.

"Glad you came?" he asked.

"Yes."

The afternoon was perfect. They splashed in the water, swimming the cool depths. Sunning for a while on the beach, they soon moved beneath a wide umbrella to avoid burning.

Talk was desultory. Molly knew she dozed part of the time, but it was so relaxing she couldn't help it.

Waking, she looked at Nick, he was studying her.

"Maybe you should have slept in this morning after all," he said.

"Oh no, I wouldn't change a thing about this day. I can sleep in tomorrow, can't I?"

"If you wish. There is a catamaran going out on an excursion run early in the morning, I thought you might like that."

She smiled dreamily. He was acting just like a real fiancé—looking for fun things for them to do on a weekend away. Would he ignore her rules later and kiss her? Push for more than separate bedrooms? Molly hoped not. It would spoil everything.

Or would it?

She closed her eyes again, still smiling at the memories of Nick's kisses.

"Nick Bailey, you son of a gun. What are you doing here? I thought you never left your office."

Nick looked up and then rose offering his hand. Sam Perkins had been a friend from college days. He hadn't seen Sam since he took over the hotels after his father died.

"What are you doing here?" Nick asked, gripping his friend's hand. "I thought you never left L.A."

"You knew I got married," Sam said proudly. "And when a man's married, he can't work all the time." Sam gestured to a pretty blonde playing with a toddler at the water's edge. "That's Stephie and our boy, Joel. I want you to meet her. I couldn't believe it when I saw you in the water earlier. I wasn't sure it was you."

Nick smiled and looked at the pretty woman. For a moment his gaze was captivated by the little boy, just able to walk on his own and fearlessly toddling into the water, only to be snatched up by his mother when he faltered. They both laughed, obviously enjoying the game. She'd set him back on his feet and again he'd head for the water.

He and Sam had been on the swim team at college together. Sam then started an import-export firm in Los Angeles specializing in Asian art. He'd been the last man Nick expected to marry. He remembered how surprised he'd been when he had received an invitation to Sam's wedding. Not that he'd been able to attend. That had to be three or four years ago.

Now Sam had a son.

Nick felt a tightening in his gut. He was thirty-six and not getting any younger. As his mother pointed out all the time, his own parents had had a school-aged child by the time they had been his age.

He looked at Molly who had sat up at the greeting.

''Sam, Molly McGuire. Molly, Sam's an old friend. We were in college together.''

''Pleasure, Molly,'' Sam said, offering his hand. He glanced between the two of them, raising an eyebrow in silent inquiry.

''Molly and I are engaged,'' Nick said.

''Sonofagun!'' Sam slapped Nick on the shoulder. ''About time. This is great news. Congratulations! Molly, you're getting a terrific guy. Say, why don't you two join Steph and me for dinner. We can celebrate in style. At the Cove Restaurant, of course,'' he said, mentioning the five star restaurant in the hotel.

Nick nodded. ''At seven?''

''Great, I'll see you both then.'' Sam smiled and headed back to his wife and son.

Nick watched for a moment, then sat back on the lounger. He looked at Molly who was thoughtfully studying the family at the water's edge.

Dinner with Sam would take the edge off dinner with Molly alone. She'd been clear it was to be a platonic weekend, but Nick had trouble keeping that in mind.

He suspected she had no idea how stunning she was in that two piece suit. Her midriff was slender, her breasts full and round. Her hips were perfection. He looked away again, wondering if he needed another dip in the water to cool down.

Closing his eyes, he tried to think of something else—anything else but Molly and her golden skin, hair piled up on her head, damp and spiky, yet tantalizing. He'd like to release it, let it spill across her shoulders. Bury his face in it and breathe in the very essence of her.

But he'd honor her request. Unless she showed she wanted it changed. And if he nudged just a little to make sure she knew her mind, knew if she wanted to change the rules, what could it hurt?

"You should have just said I was a friend," Molly said.

"What?" Nick rolled his head to the side to see her. "What are you talking about?"

"He didn't have to think we were engaged," she said, lying back down. "Now he'll have questions in the future."

"Easily enough handled," Nick replied.

"Of course," she murmured, her eyes closed.

Nick had known Sam married. But seeing him with his wife and child made it real. And changed how he viewed his old friend. He suspected if he asked Sam to go carousing like old times, he'd be turned down flat.

Sam's proud look when he spoke of his wife and son went to the heart of the matter. Sam *liked* being married. Liked linking his life with Steph and Joel. Liked being half of a couple, part of a family.

Nick wondered if he'd like something like that.

Molly didn't know if the dress she'd brought for dinner was dressy enough. She had thought she and Nick would just find a quiet restaurant. She certainly had not expected to have to play the role of adoring fiancée while sharing dinner with an old friend.

Not that she minded having dinner with the other

couple. She would learn more about Nick. Round out the picture a little.

To what end? She asked herself as she gazed at her reflection. Her cheeks and nose were just the slightest bit pink from the afternoon in the sun. Her arms and shoulders looked a shade or two browner. She clipped her hair up, in a slight variation of the way she'd worn it that afternoon. Now, a few tendrils here and there brushed across her shoulders. She was deliberately trying to look as seductive as possible.

Wouldn't a fiancée want to be sexy for her intended?

Eyes sparkling, she was ready. Let Nick eat his heart out for someone who was just passing through.

She just hoped her own heart would hold up!

CHAPTER TEN

HIS reaction when she stepped into the sitting room was all Molly could have hoped for. His gaze felt like a caress. Appreciation lit his eyes. Then a sensual sexuality seemed to arise between them.

Molly tilted her chin, she would not be daunted. "I'm ready if you are."

"You didn't wear your ring," he commented.

"I didn't bring it. I didn't expect to need it."

"We'll stop in one of the jewelry stores before going to the restaurant and pick up something." He glanced at his watch. "We have time."

Molly blinked. They were going to stop off at one of the fancy jewelry stores along the hotel's shopping area and just *pick up something?*

"We can just tell them I didn't bring it."

He shook his head. "No sense giving rise to questions."

Molly assumed they would look at the expensive costume jewelry display when they entered the store a few moments later. But Nick steered them to the fine gems section. She blinked.

"A fake would work," she murmured. Just how far did he plan to take this?

"It would be just our luck Stephanie is a jeweler and would recognize a fake a mile away. Think of my reputation."

She frowned. "I doubt she'd say anything."

''Not to my face, but to Sam for sure. Then he'd mention it somewhere and pretty soon the entire West Coast would think I hadn't bought my fiancée a real diamond.''

''By that time we'd have gone our separate ways.''

''Humor me.''

Nick spoke to the elegantly attired salesclerk and soon a display of lovely diamond rings was spread before them. Molly gazed in delighted awe at the selection. If only this was for real. If only they were choosing a ring to symbolize their mutual love. A ring that would last down through all the years of their life together. A ring to be passed down to a beloved son or daughter.

Molly's eyes filled with tears. This should be a special time between two people. She wished with all her heart it was a special time between her and Nick.

''Which one do you like?'' His voice caressed her. He stood near, as if to protect.

''They are all lovely.'' She didn't ask the price. Not with one of his own employees there. A sense of relief swept through her. Of course. He would be able to return it once dinner was over. How stupid of her to think he was actually buying the ring.

''I like that one,'' she pointed to a solitaire on a plain gold band. It was simple, but to her stunning in its simplicity.

''Not this one?'' Nick picked up one. It was showy and ostentatious. Perfect for Carmen, Molly thought waspishly. But not for her.

She shook her head, pointing to the one she wanted.

In only a few moments, the clerk had sized Molly's finger and checked the ring. It was a match.

"No wait for it to be resized," the clerk said smiling at them both. She handed the ring to Nick and waited expectantly.

He looked at her, at the ring and then at Molly.

She gazed up at him, pretending it was real. Pretending he loved her. That they were embarking on a life together.

Slowly he took her hand and gently nudged the ring on, never taking his gaze from hers.

"With this ring," he murmured softly.

The tears that filled her eyes threatened to spill. She blinked quickly and tried to smile.

When he leaned closer, she closed her eyes. His kiss was tender and gentle, his lips warm against hers, pressing as if a vow.

"Congratulations and best wishes," the saleswoman said.

Nick told her to send him the bill. She nodded, smiling broadly. He suspected she couldn't wait until they left to start telling the world he'd bought his fiancée's engagement ring at her store!

Molly was quiet as they headed for the restaurant. Nick glanced at her, wondering what she was thinking. The tears in her eyes had surprised him. Was she regretting he wasn't another man? Or that this was only a pretense?

He would have thought she'd be delighted to flaunt an expensive ring. Yet she'd chosen a simple one. It looked nice on her hand. Maybe when they were no longer engaged, he would let her have the ring.

Nick felt a sense of quiet satisfaction at the thought of Molly keeping his ring.

Nick spoke quietly to the maître d' at the restaurant and he quickly showed them to the table where Sam and his wife awaited. Introductions were made as Nick and Molly joined them. Soon dinner had been ordered and conversation began.

Sam was curious about Nick's engagement. When he learned it was recent, he flagged the sommelier and ordered champagne. He had a million questions, which Nick tried to answer as vaguely as possible. When the chance arose, Nick steered the discussion to Sam and his own marriage. On that, Sam was verbose. Stephie was friendly and amused by her husband's sweeping commendation for marriage, finally reining him in and deftly changing the subject.

Nick watched the interplay between his old friend and his wife. They were obviously well suited and enjoyed being with each other. The memories they already shared excluded others. Was that a part of marriage he hadn't considered? Being part of a team, a couple, who built memories only the two of them shared? Creating a world of their own?

He flicked a quick look at Molly imagining them over the months and years ahead. He was attracted to her on a very primal level. Yet he had never considered marriage. When he was ready, would he want someone like Molly? Want Molly?

The champagne arrived and toasts were made. Nick shook off the pensive mood and enjoyed the couple sharing dinner with them.

The evening sped quickly by. Making vague promises to get together before too long, the two couples said good night at the elevators. Molly and Stephie exchanged hugs. They had had plenty to talk about all evening, Nick thought. He was more wary about starting new friendships, not so Molly.

"They are nice," she said as they rode the elevator to their floor. "And Sam is so funny. I bet they laugh a lot in their household."

"He liked tonight's audience."

"Umm." She grew quiet.

"Tired?" Nick asked.

"Yes, a bit. I think that sunshine and fresh air really takes a toll. Not that I don't want to go to the beach tomorrow."

"Sleep in if you like. We'll hit the beach whenever you are ready. Our flight home isn't until late in the afternoon. Plenty of time to spend on the beach."

When they reached the suite, Nick opened the door letting her in before him. She passed so close, he could breathe in her sweet scent. He followed, shutting the world out when he closed the door.

If they were really engaged, he wouldn't let the evening end just yet. Did Molly want more?

She stopped in the middle of the sitting room and looked around at him.

"Thank you for today. I had a great time."

"I did, too." He came up to her, reaching for her. When she came willingly into his arms, he kissed her. He'd been wanting to touch her all night. Not the casual brushes of fingers against her arm, but hold her, touch her, kiss her until neither of them could think straight.

And for him, it wouldn't take long. She was a delightful armful of femininity that had his senses reeling. Her mouth was sweet and responsive. Her tongue touched his, mated with his, feeding the primal desire that built. Her taste was special, one he couldn't get enough of. The soft murmurings as she pressed against him were driving him crazy. She was hot and exciting and willing.

Slowly he moved toward his room. They could end the night together and in the morning—

Nick met resistance. He lifted his head and looked at Molly. Her cheeks were flushed, her eyes sparkling with passion. Her lips were rosy and slightly swollen from their kisses.

Her hand was pushing against his chest.

"I need to go to bed." There was no mistaking the determination and resolution in her tone.

"Come with me," he said softly.

She shook her head regretfully. "I can't. I can't."

Slowly Nick took a deep breath, wishing he could turn off his feelings as easily as she seemed to. He released her, spinning away, angry, disappointment, frustration replacing the hot passion of a moment ago.

"Good night," she said and fled.

He heard her door shut and with regret headed for the bar at the side of the room. It was going to be a long night.

Molly awoke the next morning and lay in bed a few moments remembering yesterday. She'd never been whisked away to a weekend before. And such a weekend. She glanced around the most elegant hotel room she'd ever seen. The furniture was French Provincial. The paintings on the walls were original oils, not mass reproductions. Even the carpet was thick and luscious. French doors led to the balcony that ran the length of the suite.

Rising, she crossed over and opened them. The cool morning air rushed in, billowing the lacy curtains, pressing her gown against her body. If Nick were awake, maybe they could have breakfast on the balcony. The view of the Pacific was stupendous, its deep blue waters stretched out to forever.

She grabbed a robe and went to see if Nick was awake.

Opening the door to the sitting room, Molly was disappointed when she didn't see him there. His bedroom door was opened, however. Maybe he was up and waiting for her.

She crossed the room, hearing his voice. Was there someone else here?

She paused at the door and peeked in. Nick was dressed sitting at the desk, talking on the phone.

"...thanks for the report. I'll leave the rest to the attorneys.... I haven't seen her, but I haven't even had breakfast yet.... I knew there was more to it than appeared on the surface, I never trusted her. You know I won't be bluffed by a trumped up breach of promise scam at some future date. She knew the rules going in. Let the diamond suffice in lieu of any other payment."

Molly stepped back, out of sight. Who was Nick talking to? Who was he talking about? Blood pounded in her veins as she suspected it was herself. He had never trusted her. Had questioned her motives more than once. Did he think she was going to try to bring some action against him to get money?

She leaned near the door, knowing she shouldn't be eavesdropping, but unable to help herself.

"Yeah, well that's Molly for you. Maybe you should just stay on the payroll and investigate every female I date. That way, I won't have to plan on a payoff each time I see one more than once. Diamonds aren't cheap."

Molly had heard enough. She turned and stalked back to her room. Her temper flared. How dare he think she wanted a diamond! She held up her hand and glared at the ring. Snatching it off her finger, she almost threw it out the French doors. But, prudently, she refrained. She tossed it on the bed and went to get dressed.

She hadn't asked to come on this trip, she muttered as she stuffed clothes into her suitcase. She hadn't asked to have her painting bought and displayed in hotel lobbies, she fumed as she dressed in record time. She hadn't asked to enter into some dumb engagement-of-convenience. She had only asked for one evening's pretense.

What she'd asked for, she remembered, was someone tall dark and dangerous. And Nick had proved all three. Especially dangerous to her heart.

She brushed her hair, gazing unseeingly into the mirror. He was too cynical to be believed. She had no intention of filing a breach of promise suit. Did people still do that? To tell the world someone promised to marry you and then reneged would be worse than Justin dumping her. How could anyone do that?

Maybe if they were mercenary.

Which she was not!

But maybe that's the way Nick saw her. She

paused, brush in midair. It was. Wasn't he always assuming he could buy this or that and get his way—like she was helping out just for what she could get? Slamming the brush down on the dresser, she almost went to confront the man. But she decided against it. Better to just leave. She remembered how fervently she had wished buying the ring symbolized something special—instead he saw it as payoff to buy her silence.

She had been doing a favor for his mother. But no, he had to think she was after more. Obviously Donny's preliminary investigation had not been enough, Nick had asked for more. Well he was welcome to his report. And his ring. And his stupid assumptions.

She glanced around to make sure she had forgotten nothing, picked up her small suitcase and the ring and headed out.

He was still on the phone. She placed the ring on the table where he'd be sure to see it. She didn't want theft added to the poor opinion Nick had of her.

Without hesitation, she left the suite and headed for the taxi stand. In only a short time, Molly was heading for the airport. She'd have to buy a ticket, but that was a small price to pay to leave immediately.

She felt as if she'd been slapped. She'd fallen for a man who thought she was a gold digger. She had offered to help out for the sake of a sick woman, and he'd believed she had something else in mind. How could she care for a man who thought like that?

Yet she did. The ache in her heart was almost overwhelming. She wouldn't see Nick again. And the thought almost brought her to tears. She loved him.

Molly took a flight to San Jose, and headed for her parents' home. They were still on their cruise. She'd check the mail, water the plants, and stay in her old room. It was hiding out, but she didn't care.

She'd call into work tomorrow and take a personal day. Or maybe use some of her vacation time and take the whole week off. And stay away from Nick Bailey!

CHAPTER ELEVEN

BY THURSDAY, Molly was going stir crazy. She had weeded her mother's flower beds, dusted and vacuumed the entire house, caught up on some reading and visited with each of the next door neighbors. But she was unhappy and bored.

She dreamed of Nick at night and thought about him endlessly during the day. Keeping busy didn't drive his image from her mind. She had memories galore from the fun at the beach, to their day at the wharf, to meeting his mother, to seeing childhood pictures and hearing his childhood antics.

But she would get through this. She'd only known the man for a few weeks. In no time, she'd get over this silly infatuation and be back on an even keel. Every time the phone rang, she would not expect it to be Nick. Every time she heard a car in the street, she would not expect it to be Nick.

Maybe she was making more about this than warranted. Had he even tried to reach her once he returned to San Francisco? Or had he understood by her leaving the ring that their time was ended?

She wondered what he had told his mother. Or was he continuing to pretend so she would recover faster?

When the phone rang Thursday afternoon, Molly was tempted to let it ring. Her parents had an answering machine. But all their friends knew they were still away. And Molly had given this number to her boss.

''Hello?''

''Molly, this is Brittany. I do hope everything is all right.''

Brittany! ''They are, why shouldn't they be?'' Why in the world would Brittany be calling her? And how had she gotten Molly's number?

''Well, you haven't been at work all week, which is so unlike you. And Nick has been here every day, looking for you. Obviously there's trouble in paradise. Is there anything I can do?''

Molly gripped the receiver tightly. As if! ''Nick has been there?''

''Every day—but he does vary his times. He just left. I'd say he was desperate. I told him I'd see what I could find out for him.''

''How nice of you to volunteer,'' Molly wanted to grit her teeth. She knew why Brittany had volunteered—more gossip! ''Sorry, I've got to go.'' Molly hung up. She couldn't believe Brittany had called. Seeking information for the gossip mill, she knew. But was what she said true? Had Nick been to Zentech every day?

The doorbell sounded.

When Molly opened the door, she sighed. ''I should have known. What took you so long?''

Donny smiled. ''I do have other clients. But Nick's my cousin. He tried it on his own, but I had a hunch. Can I come in?''

Molly hesitated, then shrugged. What did it matter if Donny came in or not. He knew where she was. Her safe haven was gone.

She led the way into the living room, sitting on a chair and motioning to the sofa. Donny sat on the edge and looked around, then at her.

"Want to tell me why you ran out like that."

"Does it matter?"

"Not really, but it doesn't seem in character."

"From your extensive investigation?"

He narrowed his eyes. Despite the coloring difference, for a second, he reminded her of Nick. "I thought we were past that. We didn't want to introduce a total stranger to Aunt Ellen."

"I mean the recent one," she said.

He shook his head. "You've lost me. There was only the one, quick and dirty the day after the Zentech reception."

She studied him for a moment. Doubt came. "I heard Nick talking with you on Sunday."

"I brought him up to date on the embezzlement. Turns out there were two involved. Nick plans to prosecute both."

"There was more to the conversation—I heard him talk about a diamond."

Donny nodded.

"Well, then, that's why I left."

He frowned. "Why?"

"I just told you."

"You're mad because Carmen's keeping the diamond pendant he gave her for Christmas?"

"Carmen?"

Donny nodded. "Nick's looking for you. He didn't know why you left. He's tried Zentech, your flat."

"Then sicced you on my trail?"

"No, this is what you call taking initiative. If it didn't work out, I didn't want to get his hopes up."

Molly was confused. What hopes? Why would Nick care one way or another—except for his mother. And his own desire to be in charge, to make sure things were going just as he wanted.

She looked at her hands, then back up at Donny.

"It was a fake engagement. You know that. I never met him before that night."

"So? I think he cares about you. Maybe more than he knows. Your leaving shook him up."

"It wasn't intended to. Just to —" She closed her mouth before she could say too much.

"Well, for what it's worth, I think he'd sleep better at night if he heard from you. Or saw you. Give the guy a break, Molly. And see where it leads." Donny rose and gave a half salute. "I'm heading back home. This San Francisco living is too much trouble for an L.A. guy."

She watched him leave, wondering how long before he called Nick.

When the afternoon passed and no phone call came, Molly began to believe Donny had not told his cousin where she was. If he hadn't, why not?

I think he cares about you, Donny had said.

As she tossed in bed that night, unable to sleep, different images of Nick once more rose to mind. Then one scene crept in—when he'd bought her a ring. "*With this ring...*" he'd said. Just as if it were for real.

She sat up. What if Nick was falling for her? What if she was spurning the very thing she wanted more than anything in the world?

How could she find out?

She could ask him.

She plopped back on the pillows. Right, she had a life-size picture of her sauntering up to Nick and saying, "I love you, how do you feel about me?"

He'd probably laugh in her face, if he didn't accuse her of trying something to get his money. Honestly, the man was fixated about that.

And why not, if all the women he met were in it for one thing.

She wasn't, but did he know it? She'd wanted his help that first night. But that was all. And he'd asked for hers the next day. Which she'd given freely—though he was always talking about compensating her.

Except, he'd stopped that recently. Was he seeing her differently?

"With this ring..." His voice echoed in her mind. She had so wanted it to be real. But she had not imagined him saying that. Why would a hardened businessman be given to romantic fantasy? Just to play the part in front of a salesclerk? She didn't think so.

Molly sat up again, and looked at the clock. It was ten minutes after midnight. Too late to go anywhere tonight.

"He'd sleep better knowing where you are."

Was Nick having trouble sleeping, or was that Donny's way of saying he was concerned where she was.

More than concerned if he showed up at Zentech every day. How awful for him, to have to admit to people he didn't know where she was. He'd said once if someone wanted something enough, it was worth any risk. Was he taking a risk for her?

How badly did she want Nick Bailey?

She switched on the light and reached for the phone. Trying directory assistance, she struck out. Not that she really thought his number would be listed. And he had never given her any phone number. Wouldn't people who were interested exchange phone numbers?

Finally she tried the hotel.

"Nick Bailey," she said when the phone was answered.

"Whom may I say is calling?"

Molly blinked. She had thought of a voice mail or something. Was he still at work at almost twelve-thirty at night?

"Molly McGuire."

"Hold please."

"Bailey." His voice sounded the same. She closed her eyes, savoring it.

"Hi Nick, it's me, Molly."

There was silence on the other end for a moment. Then, "Where the hell are you and why did you take off like that last Sunday?" The harshness in his tone surprised her.

"I'm at home. I didn't mean to make you worry."

"What did you think I'd do when you weren't there? I thought at first you'd been kidnapped. Then someone said they'd seen you get into a taxi and head for the airport."

"I, uh, overheard your conversation on the phone and misunderstood."

"What are you talking about."

"It's sort of a long story. I'd be happy to tell you tomorrow. That is, if you still want to see me."

"Yes. Tonight. I can be at your place in ten minutes."

"I'm not at my flat, I'm at my folks' place. I'll return to San Francisco tomorrow. We could meet—"

"Where is the house? I'm coming there tonight."

"It's in Fremont. Good grief, you can't come all the way out here tonight. It's already after midnight."

"I'm awake and you're awake, what does the time matter? Give me directions."

As soon as she hung up, Molly flung off the covers and dashed into the bathroom. Nick was coming here tonight. She had forty-five minutes or so to shower and get dressed. She couldn't believe he wouldn't wait until tomorrow. She could have explained then. Or even over the phone.

But he insisted on seeing her tonight!

Molly was watching from the living room window when the car turned into the driveway. She ran to the front door throwing it wide as he got out of the car. Watching as he walked quickly up the walkway her heart pounded.

He saw her and quickened his pace.

"Don't you ever do that to me again!" he said, sweeping her into his arms and holding her so tightly Molly couldn't breathe. Before she could say a word, his mouth covered hers in a searing kiss.

Molly clung for dear life, feeling the anger in the kiss, but the relief and something else. Guilt assailed her. She had never meant to worry him.

She gloried in his embrace, relishing every inch of

him she could reach, holding on tightly as she returned his kiss, deepening it when he did, wishing the moment would go on forever.

It did not, however. Slowly he eased his hold until he pulled back enough to look into her eyes.

"Your explanation had better be plenty good."

She touched his cheeks, seeing the worry still lingering in his face. "You look tired," she said.

"I've barely slept since Saturday night. Why did you leave like that?"

"I thought I had a good reason. Want to come in and hear it?"

He glanced around the darkened neighborhood. No other people appeared to be up, but there was no reason to hold their conversation outside. "If you insist." He released her and stepped back. They entered the house and Molly led the way to the living room. She sat on the sofa, Nick right beside her.

"If you want something enough, it's worth any risk," she said. "Do you remember telling me that."

He frowned. "I may have said something like that."

"Sometimes risks can be scary."

"What does this have to do with San Diego? You were scared there?"

"No. I was happy there. I had a wonderful time."

"That's why you left like you did Sunday morning?"

"Actually I overheard your conversation with Donny. Or part of it, at least. And I thought you were talking about me."

"We were talking about the embezzlers."

''And Carmen, Donny said.''

''You've talked to Donny?''

''He was here. I thought he'd tell you.''

''When was he here? And why didn't he tell me?''

''He was here today and I haven't a clue why he didn't tell you. But he told me you two were talking about Carmen.''

''And you got in a snit and left?'' His look was incredulous.

''No, I said, I thought you were talking about me. That you expected a breach of promise suit or something and would pay me off with the diamond ring you'd just bought. I thought I'd been insulted and got mad and left.''

He shook his head, anger flaring. He stared at her for a long moment, then slowly the anger began to fade.

''I thought we agreed to keep this engagement going.''

''Until your mother was better.''

''Or until we had a good reason to end it.''

''Like you met someone else?'' she asked. She didn't remember that aspect.

''Or you did.''

Not likely, not any time soon. Nick filled her senses and her mind. She couldn't even see other men for him. Risk. Take a chance.

''I might never find anyone else,'' she said daringly.

''I might not, either.''

She held her breath. What did that cryptic comment mean?

''So the engagement would never end.''

"Or we could end it like engagements normally end," he said softly.

"Huh?"

"In a wedding."

She stared at him, hope blossoming in her heart. She was almost afraid to ask for fear he'd laugh and tell her he was just teasing. But she was feeling daring tonight.

"As in our wedding?" she clarified.

He nodded, his gaze never faltering.

"As in marriage?" she said, feeling as if the room was spinning. She reached out to touch him, to ground herself.

"As in I love you Molly. I want to marry you. I want this engagement to be real until your parents and my mother can see us get married. Then we'd live together forever."

"Oh wow."

"That's all you can say?"

"I'm shocked. I was taking a huge risk, you see."

"Seems like I took the risk. You haven't said yes or no."

She laughed and flung herself into his arms. "Yes, yes, yes. A thousand times yes. I was going to tell you I love you. I was going to risk being dumped again, being made a fool of, everything, to tell you. And you beat me to it!"

"You love me." He said it with satisfaction.

"I love you. Adore you. That's what you wanted, isn't it, adoration?"

"Yes it is. You have captivated me."

She gave him a sweet kiss. "I've never captivated anyone before."

"Since that first night, I've been captivated. I didn't recognize it, then fought it. But your leaving changed everything. After seeing Sam and Stephie together, I began to think I might want something like that. Before I could put two thoughts together about it, you were gone. And I realized what living without you would be like. Not something I want."

"Which reminds me, Brittany called today. She said you'd been at Zentech every day."

"You and Brittany are now friends?"

"Hardly. She was looking for gossip. I couldn't believe she had the nerve to call. Were you really there every day?"

"Looking for you. I thought I was being subtle."

Molly laughed. "I can imagine." She took his face between her palms. "I'm sorry I ran out like that. And for the wrong reasons, too. If I had had a clue how you felt—"

"How do you think I felt—I bought you an engagement ring."

She nodded. "I should have picked up on that. You said, with this ring..."

He reached into his pocket and pulled out a small box. Flipping it open, he held it out. "I brought it. Did you really like it, or was it for show for Sam and Stephie?"

She looked at it, and then at the man she loved. "The entire time we were there, I was wishing it was for real. And when you said those words, my heart melted."

"You were in tears. I'll always remember," he said. He took the ring from the box and placed it once more on her finger. Once again, he sealed it with a kiss. Once more she gazed at the man she loved through tears of happiness.

"I love you, Nick."

"I love you, Molly McGuire."

Tall, dark and dangerous had been the perfect thing to order!

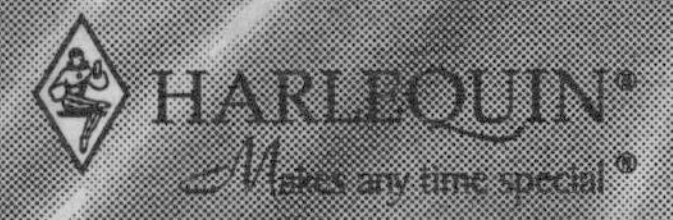
HARLEQUIN®
Makes any time special®